The Silence

Kara Ireland

A note to my readers:

  I owe you a thank you. I owe you more than a thank you, I am indebted to each and every one of you that stumbled upon my writing on Wattpad and decided to give it a chance. I owe you my success. I owe you my talent. I would have never written again, had you not encouraged me. Because of you, I have come a long way from where I started. Because of you, I have cultivated this talent you've convinced me that I have. Because of you, I picked that pen back up. Because of you, I am the writer I am today. And I cannot thank you enough.

Anna

She was back.

This was the fourth week in a row she was out there. For the past month, daily and without fail, she would come in, browse around, buy a random CD, and proceed to sit on the little wooden bench perched just outside of the shop.

I work at Small Wonder Records, a small music store that sells a variation of music paraphernalia. I'd been working there for the summer, and much of the one prior. Staying with my dad in Savannah during yet another summer since my parents' split, I jumped at the opportunity to work at the place I spent most of my childhood. I'd been employed there throughout the entire summer since I'd turned sixteen. I loved the area because of the quiet, reserved town it was in the midst of. Our store didn't get a lot of activity, with the exception of that girl.

It's sort of an old, vintage kind of store – but that's what I like about it. Although it is sparingly, our collection of records and CDs attracts very diverse people, like that girl.

Typically, I wouldn't pay much attention to the passing wayfarers the store draws in. People constantly come and go, filtering through those double doors for a few minutes and then carrying on with their lives. I don't bat an eyelash. We don't get many returning customers, people check us out and they're on their way. This place practically survives on hipsters, or wannabes – for that matter. However, that girl makes it a point to fit us into her daily schedule. That was a factor that begged scrutiny, eventually.

After the first week of noticing her daily presence, I started to look forward to seeing a familiar face. That was at the beginning of last summer. Most of the time, she wasn't alone. She used to come in here with a boy a few years younger than she was. Together, they'd sit and talk right outside the shop. But he'd stopped coming. Maybe he'd gotten too old to hang out with his sister or something, I never knew. I assumed they were siblings, because they resembled each other quite a bit. I could always count on the pair stopping by. However, the recurring habit ceased for a while – I didn't see her for the last couple of weeks. Shortly after that, I moved back across the state to be with my mom in Atlanta again. When I began working there again the following summer, she'd reappeared and had fallen back into that peculiar habit. And there she was today.

She was so peculiar to me, so mysterious. Unlike others who the sun had merely been kind to, she was always this lovely shade of brown no matter the climate. She was a stunning black girl. She looked about my age, maybe a bit older. She always wore a grey beanie that hung halfway off of her head, exposing her widow's peak. Underneath the beanie, she had very pretty, loosely curled, dark brown hair that nestled around her shoulders. There wasn't a day that went by that I didn't see the girl with that nice, caramel complexion sauntering in.

Usually, she'd be donned in some variation of tee shirt and jeans. I'd noticed that she liked to keep it casual. Without much jewelry or anything very flashy at all, she'd come in and browse our selection. Much like I did with everyone else, I would watch her milling about the store. However, with her, I always seemed to stare longer; have more trouble diverting my gaze. She was sort of beautiful, to me anyway. To most people, she was probably just another girl. To my coworker, Cassie, she was probably just another customer. To me, she was captivating.

In my day to day scrutiny, I noticed something new about her. My attraction towards her grew daily. Gazing impassively at her from my usual position at the counter, I always took in her little details. While she was browsing the store, she'd always ruffle her hair. She messed with her hair a lot, usually removing her beanie to do so unnecessarily. When she came up to the counter to buy her album of choice, I took those moments to scan over her face. When I came across beautiful things, I liked to indulge.

She was familiar to me, but there was always something more to notice. When I could steal a glance, I made note of the faint spots of acne on her cheeks. Nothing that diminished her looks, however. I found that there were hardly noticeable freckles dotting her nose and sprinkled across her cheeks – and there were only a few. I could only ever see that when she ducked her head to retrieve her money. Up close, I registered her bushy eyebrows. Bushy as they were, they were plucked with such overwhelming artistry. Everything seemed to suit her so well. She hardly wore makeup, and for that I was grateful – she was gorgeous as is. She was no show–stopper, no manifestation of some Hollywood projection at all. But she was real. She had authentic beauty, and I liked that about her.

She was a quiet being, too. I could only ever notice the physicalities because she never offered much conversation.

I'd always seemed to take a liking to people with stories, and she seemed to have a damn good one. Everyday she came by, she never spoke. Instead, she just offered that same half–smile as compensation. And it was odd. In my usual interaction with my customers, I'd comment on whatever they'd bought – a friendly observation more often than not. They'd reply, pay, thank me, and go on about their day. My day went by faster when I made people smile with my witty commentary. And I always made her smile, but I never made her talk. That was bothersome. I'd made several remarks about the artists she'd chosen or reminisced on the concerts of some I'd been to with her, expecting conversation to follow to some extent.

It never did.

I'd been ignored by many people. My hello's weren't always returned. My smiles were met with blank faces often. Some of my questions of their opinions went unanswered at times. It was the price you paid for working in customer service. That wasn't what bothered me. But the familiarity I was getting to have with her was getting under my skin. Every day I would see her, and I never knew anything more about her by the time she left. I didn't even know the girl's name. All I knew – and all I would ever know, I presumed – was which artists she was fond of. That wasn't nearly sufficient enough for me.

Each day after ringing her up, I would cast a glance outside of the shop's window to see her sitting there on the bench. She wasn't a *total* weirdo, she usually brought things to occupy herself. I might've had a sociopath on my hands if she just sat on the bench with no motive. But usually, she had a book to read or a notebook to write in. My initial guess was that perhaps she had no home to return to, but I quickly overruled that inference because she seemed well kept. I was completely perplexed by her odd routine, so today I just decided to ask her.

"$11.89," I informed her as I rung up her album. Today, she'd picked up *The Way It Was* by Parachute. I'd grown to notice her liking for bands over the time she'd been coming here. This was a nice selection for today. As usual, she smiled and paid silently.

When she turned to walk away, I reached over the counter and brushed her shoulder lightly. "Hey, why do you always sit out there?"

I'd asked it tentatively, but it still sounded abrupt. Too abrupt for my liking. This was our first interaction, and I'd just asked a rather probing question. Couldn't I have started with a '*how's your day?*' I blanched at my forwardness and hoped for the best.

In response, she shrugged simply and walked away. I furrowed my eyebrows in confusion, wondering why she'd ignored me. I had half of a mind to follow her, but decided against it for fear of making her uncomfortable. My chances for today were already botched. I'd just ask her tomorrow.

The next day, I tried a different approach. Today's album was *Everything's Fine* by The Summer Set. I rung it up, though she already knew the price. All albums always came up to be $11.89, only the newer albums and deluxe versions of albums were more expensive. She hardly ventured into those, though.

"Hi. So, I noticed you come in here every day..." I offered her an inviting smile as she fished through her wallet for the money. The unnamed girl smiled and nodded slightly. That at least warranted a '*yeah*', if not an explanation. I was thrown for a loop, why wasn't she talking?

"What's your name? I'm Anna," I said casually in a second attempt to start conversation. She held up one finger, indicating that I should wait. She whipped out a pen, and my coworker called me from the back. I turned around to see what she wanted, but she waved me off, having apparently changed her mind. When I turned back around to face the beanied girl, she was gone.

I directed my attention to the door just in time to see it closing. She was strolling down the sidewalk with her new album in hand. Bemused, I rested my chin in the palm of my hand. Well, that was frustrating. I noticed she'd simply left her payment on the counter and I picked it up to stash it in the register. It was the habitual $11.89, left in exact change. Once I put the money in the register, I noticed writing on the ten–dollar bill.

Jamie was written in small, girly script on the bottom left side. I ran my finger over it with a grin before shutting the register. As small as it might've been, this was the first step to unraveling the mystery that is Jamie. With that knowledge, I was sated.

Anna

I loved challenges. Getting to know Jamie was one of them. Her way of telling me her name yesterday was all I thought about that night and most of the following day. It disheartened me that she hadn't spoken, but her creative way of divulging her name struck me as awfully cute. I was determined to get a little bit more out of her today. When she came by, I greeted her by name.

"Hi, Jamie," I grinned across the store as she entered.

In response, she gave me a smile that reflected her surprise, accompanied by a subtle wave. Still no words, but I wasn't going to be discouraged yet. She then walked off to begin her search. It was always up in the air where she would decide to look. Her taste seemed to vary from day to day, and that was the one thing I could never quite predict about her. Our albums were categorized by genre, then artist. The genres were amongst the shelves. Random, or often misplaced, albums were scattered about in the crate in the center of the floor. Jamie had my attention as she browsed our selection. I always wondered what she found so intriguing; how after all this time, she was still so curious. Hadn't she memorized the entire store by now?

Pensively, I observed her observing our collection. She scanned each row of CDs, then each crate. She grazed each album with the tip of her finger as she looked for the one she would buy. A smile graced her lips as she picked up the chosen one. I found myself matching her expression as she read the song titles listed on the back. I stealthily averted my gaze as she approached the counter, not wanting to give the impression that she'd had an audience the entire time.

"$11.89," I smiled nonchalantly and she reciprocated with a similar quirk of her lips.

She handed me her exact change out of habit, and she waited patiently as I placed *Where the Light Is* by John Mayer in a plastic bag. I handed it to her and she thanked me, unsurprisingly, with yet another smile. She sure did smile a lot.

When I checked the time, it was twenty after six. I'd refrained from taking my break all day, just so I could possibly spend it with Jamie. I proposed the idea as I reflected on our interaction last night and I'd decided to go through with it. Something was drawing me to her, though I couldn't place what. I didn't know why she was my latest obsession. I didn't know a single thing about her, beyond her name. Yet I was completely entranced.

"I'm going on my break," I casually informed Cassie, my manager and close friend, before slipping from behind the counter.

I exited the shop and inconspicuously cast a glance at the bench. Jamie was sitting there, much like I knew she would be. I figured it would be weird if I just sat down, so I decided to go to the bakery across the street. As far as Jamie knew, I was getting a late lunch – or an early dinner. A snack, perhaps. As I was ordering, I was so paranoid about Jamie leaving. It was unlikely that she would, because under most circumstances, she only left when it got dark. Nightfall wasn't due for at least another two hours in this early June. That knowledge didn't stop me from nervously looking over my shoulder to check if she was still there every few minutes.

I settled on purchasing a stale looking bagel and a small bottle of orange juice. Just before leaving, I checked myself in the reflection of the door. I looked pretty enough. I reestablished the part in my dark–brown hair and ran my fingers through it. My eyelashes looked long today and made my dark eyes look fierce. I liked that. It boosted my confidence. My complexion was a little pale – I would've liked to be tanner, but that was beyond my control. My face looked a little flushed, but then again, it was hot outside. Whatever.

As I exited the bakery, a sense of dread washed over me. What if when I sit down, she moves? What if she doesn't want me there? What if she *still* doesn't talk to me?

In my tentative approach, Jamie happened to look up. We made eye contact, and those unnerving dark eyes left me feeling extremely flustered all of a sudden. My breath hitched in my throat, but I tried to appear unfazed as I stepped closer. I raised my eyebrows, silently asking if I could sit there. She nodded with an inviting grin and moved her small bag into her lap. She even patted the seat, urging me to sit next to her.

She was so accommodating, my nerves began to dissipate. My heartrate was coming back down as I took my seat next to her awkwardly. I was beside her. In her immediate vicinity. Because she'd allowed me to be. It was the smallest success, but a success nonetheless. With a daft smile after that realization, I looked down at my bagel and realized that I wasn't actually hungry at all.

With my head down, my hair was obstructing Jamie from view. I brushed it back and peeked over at her. Her cheeks were flushed and her hair was almost sticking to her forehead due to the heat. She had the most beautiful glow about her, and it didn't faze me that it was due to sweat. The girl was stunning and worthy of admiration. I stared for a beat too long, apparently. She sensed my gaze and turned to look at me, and I quickly shifted my gaze back down into my lap.

I wondered what exactly I was doing as I bit into the bagel. What was the plan? I'd hoped to talk to her, or something, but all we were doing was sitting here. I figured I should take initiative, because Jamie seemed unlikely. I hurried to chew my small mouthful. It was as stale as it looked, and just as bland. I grimaced and took a sip of my orange juice. Stalling. That was cool, crisp, and refreshing. Still stalling. We sat there in silence for a few minutes, which I'm guessing wasn't unusual for Jamie. It *was* strange to me, and I felt incredibly inept.

I racked my brain to think of something to say to her, but came up short. I even twiddled my thumbs for a bit, completely unsure of what to say or do. This decision was slowly proving to be redundant. I looked over at Jamie for some kind of indication that she would spark conversation. She was looking straight ahead with an impassive expression. The answer was undoubtedly no, but I couldn't help wondering what was going through her mind. I wondered if it was as beautiful as she seemed to be, as she so outwardly presented with so little effort. I knew I wouldn't be let in on her light any time soon. In my quiet assessment of her, I simply watched her watching the world. Her eyes drifted amongst our surroundings. I assumed she was people watching, so I decided to people watch too.

There wasn't much to see, this side of Savanah was pretty quiet. No one really walked anywhere anymore, but there were a few stragglers amongst the plaza across from our storefront. There was a burly man in a suit that was much too small, obviously a businessman. He went into the bakery I'd just come out of. I figured he must've been on his evening lunch break. Approaching us on the sidewalk was a mother and her baby boy. She was holding his hand as he walked a few steps in front of her. He looked so happy with his little pacifier in his mouth and his wobbly legs. He was precious. The woman smiled when our eyes met, and I turned to Jamie to see that she was smiling as well.

People watching was underwhelming because there wasn't a plethora of people to look at, yet I was still entertained. Perhaps I'd convinced myself of the latter because I was doing it with Jamie. I wanted to like what I was doing with her, even if it only amounted to sitting on a bench. And I did like it, it brought me some estranged form of joy. It gave me the strangest sense of fulfilment. I felt that I'd truly accomplished something in gaining the privilege of sitting with her here, today. It seemed that I'd lost track of time.

My thirty–minute break was nowhere near my cognizance until I caught the time on my phone and registered that I'd spent an extra ten out here. Jamie seemed to have to leave at the same time, and our eyes met as we both shuffled to get up. She grinned and brushed my hand as a gesture of goodbye. Still no words. Her light touch did make my heart flutter, though. I stood there a few seconds more to watch her walk away, and I couldn't wipe the idiotic grin off of my face for the life of me.

I sighed contentedly and pushed through the door to go back to work for another two hours. Why I was so sated from just being in her presence was beyond me. I'd yet to find an adequate reason, but I felt fulfilled, indeed. Being out there with her was refreshing, somehow. I looked back to catch one last glimpse of her before she disappeared completely. When I finally diverted my eyes and tuned back into the store, Cassie was smirking at me.

"Who's the girl?" Cassie raised her eyebrow knowingly.

"Jamie," I beamed, still reeling from our silent encounter. "You know her. She comes in here all the time."

"Yeah, she comes in here all the time. But today, you chose to sit out there with her?" Cassie prompted, and I couldn't discredit her observation.

"Yeah. I figured I could use some fresh air," I fabricated and kept my ulterior motives to myself. Apparently, they needed no announcement.

"Fresh air," she scoffed. "You like her," Cassie inferred as I took my seat on the stool behind the counter. Her smirk was so prominent, I knew denying the statement would be futile. It didn't stop me from doing so, anyway.

"What?" I breathed, and an uncomfortable giggle got past my lips. The confrontation had made me giddy, and I knew my goofy smile was only proving her point. "No, no I don't. I don't even know her."

"Not yet, but I can tell you want to," Cassie assumed smugly and leaned on the counter beside me.

Well, she wasn't wrong about that. "Of course, I do. She's like our best customer. She gives us daily business, I owe it to her to be friendly."

"Best customer," Cassie sneered at my excuse again. "You *so* like her."

"I don't, I just want to get to know her," I said as casually as I could. It was the most innocent type of attraction. I wanted to discover a real reason to like her, as Cassie so insisted that I did. The notion couldn't be discredited. She was definitely a candidate worthy of a crush, it just hadn't been properly developed.

"But you do," Cassie laughed off my denial. "Why else would you be so interested in her, then?"

"She's riveting," I shrugged, without much more room to go in depth. It strengthened my point about having no grounds to like her. I simply didn't know enough, but it was becoming my goal to do just that.

"Well, you're in luck. She looks like the kind of person that wouldn't mind the fact that you just used the word: *riveting* in real–life conversation," Cassie made fun of me and my vocabulary, like she always did.

"Shut up," I replied halfheartedly. Cassie only looked at me and shook her head, then returned to the back to finish organizing discarded albums.

Cassie's teasing provoked some thought about it. *Well, she's pretty*. I reasoned to myself. *I like her hair and her eyes. She's got a cool style, I guess, with the beanie and all. I especially like the whole beanie–in–the–summertime thing she has going on. She has a good taste in music.*

These were all simple observations. I didn't know the first thing about her, save her name. Because she didn't talk. That was the mystery of it all. I was set on unraveling it. And having that sudden compulsion wasn't exactly tantamount to liking her, but I was well on my way.

Anna

The next day, I repeated the same process. I prolonged my shift so that I could spend it with Jamie again. After she bought the album and left, I went to the bakery. This time, I chose something that at least looked somewhat appealing. It was some type of pastry in a weird shape, and I bought it along with a small lemonade. If Jamie could adopt the practice of sitting out there daily, I figured I could find my own reasons to join her. This was going to be my habit, and Jamie was going to be a part of my day. I was determined.

Today, I had a little more pep in my step. Knowing that Jamie had accepted me yesterday gave me a new bout of confidence. I was moving quickly because I wanted to spend as much time with her as I could. However, the concept of utilizing all of that time with her was daunting, in a way. Yesterday, we only had about forty–five minutes. Given the chance that we had until nightfall, I had no idea how I was going to keep her entertained. What can you do with a person that doesn't talk?

Maybe she's deaf... I mused as I crossed the street, approaching Jamie's bench. *No, she's not... Every day I tell her the price, she hears me. And yesterday when I said her name, she smiled. I know she can hear. So why doesn't she speak?*

When I made my way over to Jamie, I saw that she'd already scooted over – as if she'd been expecting me. It was a trivial thing I'd noticed in passing from day to day, but she typically occupied the middle of the bench. She never sat to either side, but today, she was. My presence wasn't off-putting to her, and for that, I was relieved yet again. The stray thought that she might've wanted me there boosted my spirits tremendously as I sat next to her.

"Hi," I smiled goofily as I looked over at her, still plagued heavily with those damned butterflies.

Of course, she just smiled and waved – like she always did. I sighed, but persisted.

"You don't talk much, do you?" I inferred and stole a glimpse at her side–profile. Each angle of her was deserving of praise.

Jamie shook her head no subtly. I even found it alluring that she was so modest with her movements. This girl had no fanfare about her. Everything about her was so low–key. The obvious humility resonated with me. She wasn't standoffish, or shy, even, she was just reserved. It made me think that perhaps she only shared herself with ones she deemed worthy of it. I wanted to rise to that level of importance. Being deprived of conversation was taunting, in a way. It gave me an even bigger desire to try. Maybe I was working towards something, after all.

"Why not?" I asked, knowing I wouldn't receive a verbal response. I figured I should've stopped asking questions that could be answered with a nod or shake of the head. Those didn't beg anyone to speak. I really thought I'd asked a question that was deep enough to elicit an explanation.

She glanced at me and pursed her lips. For a second, I thought I'd finally gotten through to her. I held my breath as I waited for the words, *any* words, to tumble out of her mouth.

I didn't know why I'd gotten my hopes up. Jamie's reaction was one of indifference. She merely shrugged her shoulders and looked elsewhere.

Well, I'd forgotten about shrugging. Shrugging was the equivalent of *I don't know* without words. Had this girl found a loophole to every interaction she could come across? It seemed so. Her lack of conversation was starting to agitate me, but I disregarded it. Perseverance was key. She couldn't ignore me forever.

"Well, I like your beanie," I blurted out, then blanched at what came out. I felt that I was making an ass of myself. Of all the things I could've said about her, I had to compliment her *beanie?* There are far more interesting things about her to address. I like a lot more about her, but I panicked. I didn't know what else to say.

I liked several things about Jamie, as little as I knew about her. Beyond the surface, I didn't have much to fawn over at all. Nevertheless, I'd taken a liking to many things about the doe–eyed babe by my side, like how soft and fluffy her hair looked daily, her cool style, her beanie – of course, her smile, her eyes – her eyes were my favorite, and her music taste... I could've said a lot of things. But I complimented her freaking beanie, like an idiot. I wanted to say more. Her appearance was charming, but there was more to her. I knew there was. I didn't want my attraction to be superficial, but she was making it difficult.

In response to the foolish compliment, Jamie smiled and adjusted it slightly. She pushed it back a little and elegantly fluffed her natural hair. I took notice of her widow's peak again, which was just barely peeking out beneath it. I was annoyed that I was focused on yet another physical thing, rather than something she'd said. Because she hadn't said anything at all. She never said anything.

The way she refused to talk to me was starting to get under my skin. It made me feel insecure. I was reconsidering my decision. I doubted making a habit of this at all. It was getting me nowhere. Then I figured that maybe it was pointless to sit out here. Maybe it was dumb to wait for her to stop by every day. Maybe she thinks I'm weird. I would know if she'd just say something. Why can't she just talk?

I succumbed to the silence and sat there for a few minutes more. Jamie was just sitting there as well. She was completely idle, just breathing. Her gaze wasn't even focused on anything in particular. There was a book acting as a barrier between us, but she wasn't reading it. It laid there on the bench just as listlessly as we both were. I found her so odd. It was almost infuriating that she didn't *do* anything, yet I was so entranced.

"Which book are you reading?" I questioned curiously, anticipating that she'd tell me the title and hopefully her opinion. I would feed off of it and branch off into the book I was currently reading. *That* was a conversation starter, if there had ever been one. It was foolproof.

Or so I thought. Jamie merely flipped it over and looked at me blankly. I felt the tips of my ears burn in embarrassment. The front of the book mimicked the back of it. It was red all around with no title. Because it wasn't a book.

"Oh, it's a journal," I deadpanned. Jamie raised her eyebrows when she nodded at the fact. I really wanted to evaporate.

But I couldn't bring myself to get up and leave. I couldn't just accept defeat like that. Walking away with my tail tucked between my legs would be more embarrassing than the awkward silence, itself. I had to be resilient, despite my lapse. Jamie was really giving me a run for my money, though.

There was a glare coming from below and I realized that it was the sun reflecting from her album. She'd purchased Billy Joel's album, *Glass Houses*. Her music taste was so eclectic. I liked that about her as well, she never restricted herself to a single genre, nor a single artist. She'd ventured into the oldies–but–goodies, rap, R&B, pop, electronic, rock, reggae, and everything in between.

"Anyway, I admire your music taste," I spoke aloud – but that, too, came out awkwardly. The only thing I was making a habit of was embarrassing myself.

Jamie turned to me with a smirk. She then ducked down and retrieved the album from the little bag, handing it out to me. She pointed to the fifth song, *All for Leyna.*

I looked at her, bemused. "Is that your favorite song from the album?"

She nodded enthusiastically. Her eyes were wide and her smile took over her features. Her essence had brightened significantly. You would've thought she was a child in a candy store.

"Can I show you one of my favorite songs?" I asked tentatively once I'd recovered from her beauty.

The silent girl nodded. I retrieved my phone from my pocket, along with my headphones. I gave the left headphone to Jamie, and I kept the right one. I plugged it into my phone, and Sara Bareilles' voice soon serenaded the two of us.

"He bends his breath around my name..." she sang, and I instantly relaxed. *My Love* was my favorite Sara Bareilles

song, and it never got old to me. I was hoping Jamie would be under the same impression.

As the song played, I gazed at Jamie – who had her eyes closed in bliss. That was really the only way one could listen to Sara. I loved how appropriate her reaction was. A few wispy hairs that had escaped her beanie were freely blowing in the wind. I smiled at her exposed widows peak, and how cute it was. I noticed those same faint freckles dotting her nose and cheeks, then realized I'd never had the pleasure of observing her this closely for this long. All of our interactions were at a safe distance. But I was here with her, experiencing her essence and all she unknowingly had to offer to me. My eyes couldn't drink in enough of her. It was the purest form of admiration. Her long eyelashes just barely brushed her cheekbones, and the corners of her mouth were turned up into a faint smile. She was such a pleasant sight. It almost made up for the silence.

She seemed to like the song, and I smiled at the feat. I'd been able to share a minute beauty with her, like she'd done with me without trying. The song rang true, Jamie was ordinary in the best way. I was staring at her so intently, when she opened her eyes, it startled me.

She appeared oblivious to my staring and instead focused her gaze up at the sunset overhead. She was distracted once more, and I stole another selfish glance at her. I wanted to take advantage of every opportunity to indulge. In my eyes, she was much more captivating than any sunset could ever be. As she watched the colors in the sky change, I watched as the sun seemed to bathe her skin. She was radiant. Her eyes reflected the light, and stunned me with a blazing sepia euphoria. Her gaze then shifted to the ground and she seemed to be deep in thought. I wondered briefly what she was brooding about, but I knew I'd never find out. She wouldn't tell me, even if I'd asked. So instead, I just watched the setting sun with my beautiful mystery girl. Then I frowned, knowing that the sunset meant she would have to leave soon.

My suspicions were confirmed when she let the song finish, then removed my headphone from her ear. She then bent down to grab her bag. Just before rising, she placed her hand over my knee and smiled at me. Her brief touch elicited a furious effusion of butterflies, and my heart leaped in my chest. My lips had parted in awe, momentarily rendered speechless from that interaction. Jamie paid me no mind as she stood up and waved goodbye. As she walked down the sidewalk, I realized she'd left a tiny notebook behind. I quickly collected it and scrambled to catch up to her.

"You dropped this," I announced, slightly out of breath.

Jamie's eyebrows raised and she took it from me graciously. I was suddenly enlightened with a great idea. If she didn't like to talk, so be it – but I've seen her write often enough. What if we could talk through notes or something? She could just write her responses, just like she'd told me her name.

As I stood there, Jamie grinned at me. She slipped her hand into mine and squeezed firmly in thanks before she turned to be on her way. The feelings her touch roused within me were hardly platonic. Maybe Cassie was right. Maybe I was falling for her without merit after all.

Anna

The following day, I'd successfully fulfilled my new habit. I'd skipped my break and worked throughout my entire shift, waiting for Jamie. Nobody usually came in here anyway, so it wasn't like I had to do much. Working through a shift wasn't all that strenuous. Our crowds didn't bring an abundance of people. It was sparse, and there was never anyone of importance to me. Nobody except for Jamie, that is. But she hadn't come yet. I nervously checked the clock about every five minutes, noticing she was late.

Jamie didn't come. I waited all day, but she never showed up. The sadness it evoked made absolutely no sense. I hardly knew the girl, but there I was: missing her. People came and went. I wouldn't ever have to see them again, and it wouldn't make any difference to me. But when Jamie didn't come, it daunted my entire mood. Most of my shift was spent sulking.

A few minutes before I had to close, I heard the familiar jingle of the front door. My head snapped up in the direction and my heart beat a little faster in hopes it would be Jamie. When I saw that familiar grey beanie, the biggest grin took over my features. My heart fluttered from the mere sight of her, and my mood increased exponentially.

"Hi Jamie," I greeted her, trying to keep my excitement at bay.

She looked up in my direction and waved with a broad smile. I registered it as her being happy to see me, too.

"I mi–" I started, but thankfully I stopped myself. *Why the hell would I tell her I missed her? More importantly, why would it mean anything to her? She surely hadn't missed me.* Jamie raised a curious eyebrow at me, expecting me to finish my sentence. I shook my head. "Never mind..."

I slipped from behind the counter and trudged over to where she was. I respected her personal bubble and lingered a few feet away from her. She was bowed, scanning the rows for her designated album. Her hair fell down and over her shoulders, obstructing her face from view. Trying to come off as impassive, I merely picked up an album to occupy myself. Jamie wasn't really acknowledging me, and I took the chance to gaze at her. It was most rewarding watching her when she was unaware, distracted in her own element. However, this time I wasn't at the proper angle to appreciate her much. That mass of curly hair was hiding her gorgeous face. I leaned against the shelf to hopefully sneak a peek of her face, but I miscalculated.

My arm missed the sill and I knocked into the shelf. It was a little farther away than I'd anticipated. In my uncanny record of bad luck, it caused a plethora of albums to clatter to the ground. I stumbled, but regained my bearings just before I would've toppled onto Jamie. I made sure the hard cases hadn't attacked her in my lapse. She hadn't been a casualty, but my clumsiness had scared the living daylights out of her. Her hand flew to her heart in a startled stupor.

"God, I'm so sorry..." I mumbled as I quickly ducked down to pick up the scattered CDs.

I was absolutely mortified and internally cursing myself until I heard an unfamiliar sound. Jamie was giggling. I stopped and looked up at her. A hand was covering her mouth, and her eyes were all squinty. If I'd thought she was beautiful before, I had no idea. Her laugh was easily the most beautiful thing I'd ever heard. It was raspy and warm. The butterflies in my stomach were relentless, and I was sure I was looking up at her like she was Jesus or something.

When she calmed down, she squatted to help me rearrange the albums. For the next few minutes, we worked in the silence I was slowly growing accustomed to. That was partially due to me not trusting myself to speak, as I'd only been embarrassing myself. But it was mostly because I was trying to keep my composure. Jamie's presence elicited foreign feelings, and I didn't know how to cope with it. She made me sillier, clumsier, and more nervous than what I was used to.

As we narrowed it down to only a few albums left unshelved, I was blindly grabbing for them. My hand touched the last one, but I soon felt Jamie's hand on top of mine. Jamie's hand was on mine. My hand was beneath hers. There was such soft tenacity between us for the two seconds we were in contact. I didn't look at her and didn't give her the chance to look at me. My breath was caught in my throat as I sheepishly pulled it away and unsteadily placed the last album amongst the others.

I stood up, stretching my legs. Jamie stayed down, resuming her search. She retrieved one, and she handed it to me. I made my way back up to the counter with Jamie following suit.

"Five hundred dollars," I said casually as I rung up her album.

Jamie's eyes widened, and she giggled yet again. The lovely sound nearly made me weak in the knees, but I managed to maintain my stance. She shook her head and handed me the exact change, like she always did.

I giggled along with her and joined in her melody. Cheekily, I placed her album in a bag and handed it to her over the counter. She smiled and received it, waving slightly.

This girl is gorgeous... I sighed to attest my inward thought. In that moment, I decided that I wanted to spend as much time as I could with her. I wanted more than what I'd been afforded – what I'd been finessing from her. Perhaps I could invite her to a dinner or something. Nothing fancy or extravagant, we were only teenagers, and I only had so much money. I wanted to treat her. I rushed to come up with something as she turned to walk away. I quickly moved to grasp her shoulder lightly. Man, I had to stop touching her like that. She faced me curiously, and I nearly lost my nerve.

"Did you– Do you, uh– Do you wanna go get something?" I stuttered, losing my train of thought as I met her eyes.

Jamie's expression turned into one of confusion, and I realized that my proposal wasn't at all clear.

"Something to eat – Are you hungry?" I clarified, and I desperately hoped I didn't look as idiotic as I felt.

Jamie looked thoughtful for a second before that glorious smile returned. She nodded subtly and gestured towards the door. She led the way, and I grabbed my bag and jacket before leaving. On the way out, I simply turned off the lights and locked the door, flipping the *open* sign to *closed*. Cassie could take care of the rest, tonight.

As we stood outside, I looked around to see the possible choices. Well, there were several fast food restaurants in this plaza. I scanned over our options, considering Chick–fil–A or Moe's. Perhaps that Chipotle over there, or the Burger King right across the street. I'd just gotten my check and I wouldn't mind spending a couple dollars extra on Jamie at the Carrabba's over there. Maybe I could treat her to some Applebee's a little down the way, if she was up for it. I turned to Jamie for reference, and she looked just as indecisive as I was.

"You can choose where to go," I offered sheepishly as we stood there on the sidewalk.

Jamie bit her lip subtly, then made her decision. I merely followed in her footsteps, walking in her distorted shadow. I figured we were going to Chipotle, because it seemed that that was where she was headed. On my way over, I tried not to psych myself out of it. It would be casual. It wouldn't really mean anything. Jamie would get a meal and be on her way. I vowed to myself not to make it weird as we silently walked on over there, with just the sounds of our shoes scraping the pavement posing as our noise. If anything, the indistinct shuffling of our feet served as the most conversation there had ever been between us.

Lost in my musings, I wasn't really paying much attention to the direction Jamie was headed. Absently, we sauntered down the sidewalk and across the street, then made a right. I was deeply distracted, fascinated by thoughts of how strange it was that I'd managed to invite her to dinner without so much as hearing her voice. Jamie still hadn't said a word to me. That very girl brought me back to my senses just as I was prepared to hold the door open to Chipotle in a stroke of chivalry. Jamie's hand closed over my preoccupied wrist in a gentle endeavor to stall my advances towards the wrong place.

Slightly endeared with the act but mostly taken by surprise, I paused and turned to Jamie expectantly. "We're going to Chipotle, right?"

I pointed to the Chipotle we were right in front of, and she pointed to the neighboring Cold Stone Creamery.

"Ice cream?" I asked, figuring she'd be hungry for *actual* food. My offer was intended for dinner, but I wouldn't deprive her of her desires. She only smiled, and I laughed. "Okay, sure."

Then, there was hesitation. Those moments of uncertainty gave way to moments of gratitude, of appreciation. I got to experience the latter. Because Jamie was still holding onto my wrist, she seamlessly freed it and took ahold of my hand instead. Without exchanging any words or looks at all, I accepted her hand and laced our fingers. Although I was maintaining my collected demeanor, my heart was thumping wildly in my chest at the feat. Jamie grinned indistinctly at her choice and escorted me into the small place.

We pushed through the door, and luckily there was no line. Jamie and I walked up to the counter, and I briefly wondered how she would order when she didn't speak. Once again, I had hope that I would finally get to hear her voice – to finally get my first glimpse into the phenomenon that was Jamie. I was afforded no such thing.

Instead, I got my answer when the employee automatically began fixing her order. Apparently, she came here a lot. He started with cake batter ice cream, then he mixed in graham cracker crust with a bit of cookie dough. He finished and placed it at the end of the counter. "Everything okay today, Jamie?"

She nodded politely and stepped aside so I could order. I tried not to harp on the interaction and what it insinuated. I tried not to think about the fact that this man had probably heard her voice, at least once, when I couldn't. I tried not to think about his privilege over mine. I tried not to think about the way she was clearly capable of speaking, but just chose not to do so in my presence. I tried not to think about it, so I briskly told him my order instead. "Just cookies and cream, please."

He nodded and gave me a few scoops before setting my cup next to Jamie's. She retrieved her wallet, but I shook my head. "I've got it," I smiled as I pulled out the money to pay for both of us. Jamie smiled graciously before taking her cup and sitting at a table just outside of the ice cream parlor.

I finished paying and grabbed my cup, sauntering over to Jamie. "That looks good," I noted as I looked at her ice cream.

She nodded and shoved a spoonful into her mouth.

"How did he know what you wanted?" I questioned, because it had been nagging at me. So much for not thinking about it.

Jamie shrugged simply and resumed devouring her ice cream. I pursed my lips at the typical response. Suddenly, I remembered my grand idea from yesterday. I prayed that I hadn't left it at the shop as I rummaged through my bag for the notepad and pen. I found it, along with *two* pens. I had a cheap little ballpoint pen and one of those nice, gel pens. I decided I'd hand the nicer one over to Jamie. I scrawled something on the paper in my barely legible handwriting and slid it over to her.

Hey ツ

Jamie looked at it in confusion, then up at me with a clear smile of amusement. She grasped the notepad and the pen and wrote something, herself. My heart fluttered, seeing that she was receptive to my plan. When I saw it, the goofiest grin spread across my face. That emboldened, girly handwriting spelled out the simplest form of hello, but I was deeply smitten with it. I was enamored with her effortless stroke of the pen, and then she was finished, just like that. Clearly, she'd kept it short and sweet. I was thrilled that she was entertaining this at all.

Hi ☺

Now that I had the segue into unveiling anything I wanted, I had no clue where to take this conversation. She'd invited me to converse with her, in this strange, alternative way, yet I didn't know what to say. I had so many deep, thought provoking questions because there was such a mystery on her end, but I couldn't decide where to start. I pursed my lips as I stared down at the notepad with so much blank space – with so much room for Jamie to express those silenced dispositions. It looked like it was mocking me as I stared down at it for a few seconds more. I'd scribbled and crossed out three failed attempts at jump–starting this conversation. Ultimately, I went with a safe question that I wasn't as curious about, but one that wouldn't hurt for her to divulge.

~~So, where are~~

~~Well, what is your fav~~

~~Why do you~~

What's your name?

My name is Jamie Sage Holden.

I like that. Mine is Anna Day Labon.

Your middle name is Day? That's really cute.

"Yeah, it's Day," I laughed at her comment. "I used to hate it because it's so weird... But I like it now, though. I guess you could say that it's part of what makes me special. You don't hear that combination, too often."

Yes, you're very special.

Jamie wore a slight smile as she turned it back around to me. Her expression was infectious and I found myself smiling as well, yet again. I took it upon myself to further our conversation.

I guess we should get the basics out of the way, so, how old are you?

I'm 18.

Oh, I'm 17.

Jamie smiled at me before writing her response. I watched her write, then noticed the difference in our penmanship. My big, gawky, messy script hardly compared to her pretty handwriting. I imagined her handwriting as the visualization of what her voice would sound like. It was essentially the written equivalent. I found myself wishing this conversation was happening verbally, but I was willing to take what I could get. I was lucky to be interacting with her on some level at all. I'd just realized that when she passed the notepad back to me.

When is your birthday, Anna?

December 15th. Yours?

June 3rd.

"You just turned eighteen," I noted aloud. She nodded and scrawled something else. She then extended the notepad out to me.

Why do you sit with me everyday?

I read her question and I bit my lip. Well, that stumped me. How was I to answer that? I feared that anything I came up with would come out in a way I hadn't intended. It would be interpreted incorrectly. There was no good, safe way to answer that question. I figured I'd just ask one of my own.

Why do you buy an album everyday?

Sentimental value.

Well, I wasn't expecting that answer. What could be sentimental about something brand new?

Really? Why?

My brother...

So, that boy had been her brother. I could've suspected as much. Although he was never really the source of my scrutiny, I had noticed their similarity. Based on that knowledge, I gauged that he was maybe two years younger or so. But it provoked questions – if she was buying them for him, why didn't he come to pick them for himself anymore? What had become of him? I had just been about to articulate my thoughts, but I noticed the ellipses and got nervous. I sensed that I was venturing into sensitive territory – which was tantamount to dangerous territory. Maybe I shouldn't ask any more about that. Changing the subject was my best bet, so I asked the question that had been burning in the back of my mind since I'd met her.

Why don't you talk?

After passing it to her, I realized that maybe I could've phrased it a little more delicately. I didn't want it to seem as though I was interrogating her. My approach could have been a little more sensitive, but it was out there now. She wrote something very concise, and I was already perplexed again. Surely, that was a question worth *at least* a paragraph. Which one–word response could she come up with for that? I found my answer as soon as she moved it back in my vicinity. Not with one word, but a whopping *two*.

Elective mutism.

Can you talk though?

Yes.

So why don't you?

That's why

She'd drawn an arrow up to her previous answer, opting out of really answering it. I didn't even know what that meant. The response I settled on writing portrayed my confusion.

Oh

So why do you sit out here everyday?

You're interesting to me.

Ive never even spoken to you before.

I know. That's why.

You're odd.

As she passed it to me, she was smiling. There was relief. I giggled as I wrote my response.

So are you. Do you think it's weird that I sit with you?

Yes.

Do you want me to stop?

I nervously scrawled it out and passed it over to her tentatively. I wouldn't have been prepared if she'd said anything other than no. Thankfully, that was exactly what she'd said.

No.

I smiled as I read her reply. I was sure the relief was once again evident across my face.

Then I'll sit out here every day until you don't want me to.

Okay :) Do you think its weird that I don't talk?

Yes.

Maybe I will one day.

Is it just me that you don't talk to?

No.

Do you talk to anyone?

Not anymore.

I was completely bemused. She'd told me the reason, elective mutism, but that was something I'd have to look up later. It didn't give me much room to ask more, because I couldn't even decipher what she'd already given me.

Did you like the song I showed you yesterday?

Yes, My Love is one of my favorite songs.

You knew it already?

Of course.

Really? I thought I was sharing a secret gem.

There are no secrets, just gems, when it comes to me and Sara Bareilles.

Good point. She's definitely in my top 3 singers.

I agree. She was my first concert, actually.

Mine was The Cheetah Girls...

I wrote back to her, full of delight, giggling at the contrast. Jamie laughed too, then nodded her approval. She took to writing again and this time, it was a little lengthier. I was pleased to find that she was opening up a bit.

That is so cute. I just got to experience mine not too long ago. I saved all my money to see her at the Variety Playhouse down in Atlanta. I had to travel to make it happen, and I'm so happy I did. It was one of the best nights in my life.

You were there? God, I kick myself every day for missing her. I could've gone, but I didn't. And she hasn't been on tour since. I guess that's what I get.

It was phenomenal.

I watched the videos. I cried.

Jamie laughed that same laugh that kept plaguing my stomach with those unwanted butterflies, then gave me a response that made me laugh, too.

I cried, too.

How was it?

I scribbled, then felt the need to elaborate. I took for granted how easily I could switch to verbal conversation, because Jamie was dedicated to that notepad. "Well, wait. Obviously, I know it was amazing, but like, *how was it*? Where were your seats? Did you go with anyone? What were the highlights? Like, tell me about it. I can't believe you were actually there."

Jamie heard me and seemed to have humored me. She took the notepad from me and instantly recounted her experience. This was even longer than her last entry. Finally, I'd asked the question worth responding to. And boy, was she giving me an answer. Jamie wrote so much that she'd taken up the entire page and had to continue onto the next. I watched her spill ink with that reminiscent smile on her face, knowing the same expression was present on my own. The nature of my smile was entirely different, however. I was smiling because I was getting to know Jamie, after all. Sitting on the bench in silence had brought me to this moment. I was afforded with this because of my persistence. I couldn't help thinking that this was just the beginning. I was going to hear her voice, soon. I turned my attention back to her current enthrallment and was honored to be let in on her memory.

    Well, I went with my best friend at the time. It was my junior year. We went with her mom and we drove for 4 hours to Atlanta. That was one of the best road trips I've ever been on. We laughed so much. We were so carefree and happy because we both loved Sara so much and we'd never been to Atlanta before. Well, I hadn't. Anyway, we had like 4th row seats in the middle. And it was great because they were elevated and Sara was like right in front of us. She actually picked my friend to ask her a question and it was so cool because I can say that she looked right at me, too. Technically. I was next to her and all. ~~And my favorite part~~ The part I'll never forget was during "King of Anything" where she split up the crowd into 3 parts and asked us to sing. That was just amazing. I had chills. There was a sea of people all coming together and singing with their favorite singer and it was just so amazing. I could go on for hours, I remember everything from that night. But I won't bore you with those details. Those are just the highlights.

    That sounds like a dream. Now I'm jealous of you. And now I'm kicking myself even more for not going.

    When she's back in town, we'll go together. How's that?

I would love that.

I was proud of myself for responding so coolly, so casually. I had no idea how I'd managed, when Jamie had just invited me to a Sara Bareilles concert (in theory.) I was getting better at not outwardly conveying those show–stopping moments. Most things happened internally. I had the crazy notion that I might creep her out if I squealed the way I wanted to. Nevertheless, I continued to pioneer our talk.

I love your music taste. You get bonus points for knowing Sara. I wanna see what else we have in common. What are some of your favorite artists or songs?

Apparently, this was a question worth responding to in depth as well. It brought a smile to my face how instantly she'd transformed and took to answering me. I'd roused a real response out of her again. The sun was already mostly beyond the horizon, but light was provided by the store. I was so fond of watching her jot down things on that list. I felt special that she was taking the time to do this for me. Jamie ended up writing until it was completely dark, due to Cold Stone closing. The only light was coming from the streetlights down the road and dimly lit storefronts. She couldn't see the notepad anymore. With a sigh, she set the pen down and handed me the notepad.

I gazed at it, trying to decipher her script in the relative darkness. I strained to read song title after song title, until Jamie pushed back her chair and stood up. I squinted up at her, and she pointed to the bottom of the page.

I have to go. I'll see you tomorrow, Anna.

I read it and I smiled sadly up at her in resignation. She reciprocated my warm smile and leaned down to kiss my cheek before leaving. Her silhouette didn't last long, and she disappeared. My cheek tingled. I stayed seated momentarily, grazing the skin that her lips had just touched. Where her mouth had been. Where she'd kissed me. I felt frozen, unsure of how to act. Although she was gone, I felt like I should react anyway.

"Yeah, I'll see you tomorrow..." I responded goofily to no one as I finally got up and made my way home.

Jamie

Anna was a peculiar character to me. Why she actually awaited my presence, *every day*, was beyond me. But I was grateful. No one had paid much attention to me after Corey died, but she did. She made me feel important, *wanted*, like I used to feel before he was gone.

Over the summers, we used to come to Small Wonder together. Since rediscovering my old CD player I had in my childhood, Corey was so fascinated with CDs. Born in the age of MP3 players, music apps, and Bluetooth, he had a certain appreciation for gadgets slightly before his time. He thought it was cool because it was "vintage". He wanted to use mine, often. The old thing had a few scratches on it, and it skipped every now and then, but it worked fine nonetheless. I gave it to him until I could set aside enough money to buy him his own. I wanted to get him one of quality, not the cheap kinds I'd seen when I looked around. It was going to be a surprise. He would've been so happy.

We went almost every day, because Corey loved music and I needed an excuse to get out of the house. I would accompany him on the walk from our house to the modest plaza. Most of the time, we wouldn't buy anything. Together, we were experts at browsing over things we had seen several times before. I hardly had a personal interest in this skimpy shop, but Corey absolutely adored it. I liked seeing the joy it brought him. I liked seeing the smile on his face. More often than not, I would just tag along on his trip because our parents didn't want him walking alone. Although he was fourteen, they figured he wasn't quite old enough for independence yet.

I was sitting on that bench while he was inside. He wanted to buy an album, but didn't have nearly enough money. I lied and said I didn't have it either, but I knew I did. Instead, I told him to go across the street and get a snack with what little money he had.

I knew I was being unreasonable and stubborn. He knew it, too, and he was understandably annoyed with me. He said something smart under his breath and I confronted him in return. We bickered, like we always did. We'd always riled each other up. He yelled at me and I yelled right back with the same unnecessary fervor, emphasizing that he should just go spend his money at the shop across the street or shut up about it, because I wasn't giving it to him. He hadn't responded. He'd simply turned to walk away from me.

He didn't want me to walk with him. When I followed anyway, he snapped at me about always treating him like a baby. I insisted at first, but let him go alone because he was so adamant about it, and because I was so annoyed with him as well. He only wanted to get a donut from the bakery across the street, and I was right there on the bench, so I allowed him to go. I watched him until he disappeared, headphones in ear and hands in pocket. I hadn't thought anything of it at all. In fact, I was happy to get rid of him for the moment. I would've never guessed the fatal, impending danger of our decisions and our timing.

When he returned, a drunk driver was simultaneously speeding down that street in a police chase. They should've nabbed that asshole earlier, and he wouldn't have struck my little brother. He wouldn't have killed Corey.

He hadn't died initially upon impact. He wasn't dismembered, nor deformed. He was bloodied and generally unconscious, and when I held him and examined him in that traumatic state, I had faith that ultimately, he would be alright. All he'd suffered from was a laceration to the head. Despite the way he began seizing in my arms, uncontrollably, *horrifyingly*, I was sure he would overcome that. Even as it passed and he went limp, *terrifyingly limp*, still in my protective hold, I was sure he would carry on – just as he always did, because he had always been so strong. I wouldn't allow myself to think that he'd just died in my arms. I couldn't.

He was then ripped from me again. The police were taking him. They crowded around us and escorted me to safety, away from my little brother. They engulfed Corey. I couldn't see anything. The paramedics were on the scene and everything blurred between that and the hospital. I refused to think that Corey lay there, *dying*. Instead, I began thinking about life with him after this, once he'd healed. I was sure he'd have a cast or two, and he would feel really cool about it – getting everyone to sign it. I was sure he'd be really excited to tell everyone about his awesome scar – bragging about it, even. I had never been so wrong before. That wound to his head served to be fatal, and the brain damage irreversible.

He lived for two days after that in a vegetative state. My brother was brain–dead before the doctors decided he couldn't be salvaged. There was no improvement, no matter what we prayed for on his behalf. He couldn't pull through. My very last memory with my brother was of me holding his hand at his bedside, incoherently whispering to him that it was okay to let go. Telling him that it was okay if he couldn't hold on any longer. Assuring him that I understood, and he didn't have to suffer anymore. Swearing to him that I was sorry. *Swearing to him that I was so sorry*. Asking him to forgive me before he crossed over. Promising that I loved him. I had no signs of acknowledgment. I never knew if he'd heard all of that. I never knew if he was aware of me at all.

It broke my heart thinking that the last thing Corey had heard me say in full cognizance was an unnecessary lie about eleven dollars. If anything, *that* was what broke me the most. I hadn't even been nice about it when he'd asked. I'd snapped at him. I hadn't used that moment to express how much I loved him, or how much he meant to me – and would *always* mean to me – or how special he was. I'd taken all of that for granted. And then I lost the chance.

Because of that, I've closed myself off from the world. I haven't spoken to anyone since the day I saw my brother's life so devastatingly ripped from him. Initially, I was shell–shocked from the trauma of seeing my younger brother getting decimated by a speeding car. Most people understood that I didn't want to discuss what I'd witnessed. I'd never admitted to the reason Corey died. I'd never divulged my own selfishness – the ultimate cause of his death. No one knew the story, beyond the few witnesses and the police report. No one knew that it was my fault. I preferred to keep it that way.

Every day, I blame myself. If I had just given him the damn money, he would still be here. So every day, I come here to buy an album for him. Maybe it's stupid, or pointless, or a waste of money to most people, but it isn't to me. To me, it's the only thing that provides a solace. I buy the album and bring my old CD player to play it at his grave. His headphones are the last thing of his that I have, my parents have locked everything else away. This is my article. And I intend to use it.

After they stopped pressing me for information with minimal luck, everyone succumbed to their grief. I was largely ignored as our parents mourned the loss of their baby boy. We all grieved in different ways. Mine was staying silent – elective mutism. My life has been a silent film no one has come to see. No one except for Anna.

I had no idea why she was so set on trying to figure me out. She wants to get to know me. I'm not just 'the girl whose brother got killed' to her, like I am to everyone else around here. In Anna's eyes, I am Jamie. Just Jamie. When I'm with her, I feel like that's all that I need to be. I don't need to be strong – she doesn't know what's happened. I don't have to enact my façade, she isn't aware of its origins. I don't have to shy away from her for asking how I'm feeling nowadays, or how we're coping as a family, or anything about Corey at all. She sees something in me that I don't understand, but I don't want to question it.

Anna was always strikingly beautiful to me, with her soft brown eyes and faded ombré hair. Her skin was fair and her frame was small. She had a rounded face and chubby cheeks. I found her adorable. Her lips were always forming a brilliant smile. Her face was always so bright and cheerful. She was the sweetest girl I'd ever known. Her soul always seemed so pure. The last thing I wanted was to taint her with mine. But every day, with every encounter, I get a little more optimistic. She made me happy, and she *kept* making me happy. I'd been growing more and more excited to see her. I liked having her to look forward to. I couldn't keep depriving her of conversation. It was all she wanted. Maybe she'll be the one I talk to after all this time. She sure had been working towards it.

When I walked through the door, her face lit up. Just like it usually did. I mirrored her nowadays, always reciprocating her broad smile and bright spirit. She waved enthusiastically at me and I waved right back at her.

"Hi Jamie," she greeted me with a grin.

I simply continued waving. And if it was even possible, her smile grew wider.

I squatted to begin my search. The last few albums I'd gotten for Corey were full of temperate indie songs, so I would try to get something a bit more eclectic for his taste. As I searched for something more towards the hip hop vibe, I felt her presence. I looked up to see that dorky smile and hopeful expression.

"Are you looking for anything in particular?" Anna wondered and tried her hand at assisting me. I shook my head no, but her smile didn't falter. "Well, can I suggest something?"

I nodded with a grin and stood up. I followed her over to the counter, where she disappeared behind it. She popped back up with an album in hand of someone I'd never heard of.

"Jon McLaughlin," she smiled as she extended it out to me. "He was one of *my* favorite concerts."

I graciously took it and examined the track list on the back. It seemed decent enough, although I knew it must've been great if Anna had recommended it to us. I handed it back to her and she furrowed her eyebrows.

"You don't want it?" she asked dejectedly.

I quickly nodded and reached into my purse for emphasis.

"Oh," she breathed as she visibly relaxed. "No, I was giving it to you. You don't have to pay me..."

I pursed my lips and retrieved my wallet anyway. I placed my exact change on the counter and she looked at me incredulously. "Did you hear me?"

I nodded simply, but nudged the money towards her with purpose. She sighed and rung up the album, which came to be the same price it always was. Anna begrudgingly stashed the money in the register and placed my album in the little bag. I then waved goodbye to her, although I had a feeling she'd be following me to the bench anyway. She always reminded me of a puppy when she did that, scurrying after me so I wouldn't get away. Surely enough, Anna fell into step behind me.

I'd caught on to what she was doing a few days after she'd began. The trip to the bakery was nothing but a ploy, an excuse for sitting there with me. I'd always known she'd never really gone for the taste. Lately, she'd given up on the unnecessary trip across the street. For that, I was so grateful. She didn't know that every time she crossed that street, I held my breath and prayed for her safety. I no longer had to wait there on the bench, rigidly, for her safe return. She was safe there with me.

I usually visited his grave after leaving here, but lately, I'd been spending time with Anna. I didn't mind going a little later, because I really did enjoy her company. She was a breath of fresh air to me.

I turned to face her after sitting in silence for a few minutes, but to my surprise, she was already staring at me. She quickly averted her gaze and her cheeks flushed. This was the first time I'd blatantly caught her staring, but I was conscious of it most times. She liked to look at me just as much as I liked to look at her. I don't think either of us minded the extra attention, when it was coming from the other. Had it been anyone else, I probably would've become anxious from what they'd assumed about me or scoff at their invasive, pitiful eyes. But not with Anna. Everything was different with her.

I nudged her thigh gently to get her attention, and she quickly met my eyes again. I mimed writing, and she got the idea. She pulled out the same notepad and pen she'd given me the day before.

Hi

Hi. Why'd you insist on paying for the album?

I read her response, and I noted that she'd wasted no time in getting to the point today.

It's just something I have to do... You wouldn't understand.

Maybe I could?

I buy them for my brother...

"Was that so hard to say?" she offered a shy smile. I shrugged in response. Personally, I hadn't thought it answered the question. She didn't seem to notice.

I just don't want to get too close to you...

I wrote that in hopes that she would understand what I meant. I knew she wouldn't. There was no reason she would, without my explanation. No one would. But I wasn't so sure I wanted to give it to her. Explaining would make me vulnerable, and I'd successfully avoided this for that very reason.

Anna's face dropped. She reread my sentence over and over, and as her eyes darted from word to word, I saw her demeanor changing. She looked worried, nervous, and *sad*. I hated to elicit those emotions, but it would be better than getting attached to me.

"Why did you say that?" Anna finally met my eyes with an incredibly solemn expression.

I sighed and shook my head, sliding the notepad over to me. I scribbled for a minute, and I hoped to explain myself to her.

I don't want you to get involved with me. I ruin everything. You're so beautiful and happy and lively, I don't want to ruin you, too.

She read my response and her eyebrows furrowed even further. Her lips were pursed as she tried to decipher what I meant.

"Okay... I can't believe Cassie told you, but I was hoping it wouldn't ruin anything... I understand, though..." Anna mumbled dejectedly.

What? I took the notepad back from her and wrote down my thought.

"I know you probably feel weird about it and stuff... And I know it's stupid. But I know it's a one–way thing... I didn't expect you to feel the same. But I don't want you to feel like you have to distance yourself from me..." she continued, but I was lost. "I'd still really like to be your friend... If you'll let me."

I don't think we're talking about the same thing...

I quickly scrawled out, and I pushed it over to her tentatively. I didn't know what she was getting at. I mean – I had an inkling, but it seemed so far–fetched in my mind. That couldn't have been the case, no matter how friendly she was towards me. Whatever it was, it was incorrect. My own demons were discouraging a friendship with her, not anything on her end. As far as I was concerned, she was perfect. I couldn't be held responsible for disturbing that.

"Wait... What are you talking about?" Anna questioned with the most adorable crease between her eyebrows. She was so cute when she was concerned.

I'm talking about myself. It doesn't have anything to do with you, I promise nothing is your fault. Please don't blame yourself.

I tried my best to reassure her through script. I couldn't have her thinking she'd done anything wrong. I slid the pad back over to her and nervously awaited her response.

"Oh..." she stuttered. "I– Um– I just thought that Cassie said something to you... But – Never mind... Um, forget what I said..." Anna mumbled as she blushed profusely. I gazed at her in confusion before dropping the subject.

I'm just really toxic, you have no idea. I don't want you to be a part of that.

Anna read it and the realization was clear across her face. She finally got it. "Wait, is this a self–depreciation type of thing?" she asked intuitively.

I shrugged, and her eyes softened. Certain things couldn't be said without words. I wasn't going for sympathy, much. The last thing I wanted was for her to pity me, but that was exactly what I got.

"It is... Jamie, I don't know why you don't speak... I looked it up, but I don't really understand what's happened to you to cause you not to talk. And I may not know you all that well yet, but I already know how lovely you are. You've probably got a huge vocabulary because I see you reading a lot. You're super nice, because you let me sit here with you all the time. You've got incredible music taste, clearly..." she said as she gestured to the album resting in my lap. She looked up at me and held my gaze for a moment. "You're so beautiful... I have no idea why you feel that way about yourself. I don't think you're toxic. I think you're amazing..." Anna rambled.

I stared at her, dumbfounded. And she concluded with averted eyes. "And I think all of that... All without ever hearing your voice."

Her next move took me by surprise. The next thing I felt were her warm arms encasing my body. She held me tightly and nuzzled her face into the crook of my neck. I reciprocated by wrapping my arms around her tiny torso. I reveled in this feeling. I hadn't been hugged in so long. I didn't know why, but her gesture threatened to make me emotional. I pulled away before it happened and I took a deep breath. It's time.

"Anna?"

Anna

"Anna?" Jamie prompted.

"Yes?" I answered naturally, but then it clicked.

My name fell from her lips, and suddenly I was very fond of it. I'd never really liked my name before, but when Jamie said it, it sounded like a poem. My name was a song, and the most beautiful sound I'd ever heard up to date. Jamie could've insulted me and I would've thought it was still the most endearing occurrence.

"You just said my name," I said in giddy realization.

Her voice was thick and raspy, and I assumed it had a lot to do with being mute for however long. Putting her vocal chords to use must've tickled her throat, because she coughed discreetly and excused herself with a meager smile. Jamie cleared her throat and spoke yet again, much to my amazement. "I did," she giggled.

"Oh my God! You're talking!" I exclaimed, and I'd never felt such excitement. I couldn't contain my smile. I couldn't quite close my mouth either, which was agape in disbelief.

"I am," she nodded with a smirk. Then her head was bowed as she cleared her throat once more. She seemed to be adjusting to using her voice again, but I didn't care how gruff she sounded. I was thrilled to hear her voice at all.

"Oh my God, this is what you sound like... Wow," I breathed as I looked at her in amazement. I couldn't wipe the idiotic grin off of my face.

"Not usually," Jamie laughed in slight disagreement, then swallowed and hummed to acclimate to the vibration within her throat. "I don't–" she coughed again. "I didn't know I would sound like this."

"You sound lovely," I promised with an open–mouthed grin. I just couldn't get over it. This was truly monumental.

"You're cute," Jamie laughed quietly, then rubbed at her throat.

The overwhelming feeling I had in the pit of my stomach built up and bubbled out of me in the form of laughter. Nothing was funny, I was just incredibly happy. "Oh my God," I stupidly reiterated with a wide grin.

"Thank you... For what you said..." Jamie said tentatively once she'd gotten a handle on the new sensations.

"Don't thank me for telling the truth," I countered as my general excitement subsided. Though I couldn't believe she was speaking, she was, and I wanted to take full advantage of it. "It's nothing."

"It was *everything* to me," she said with a certain honesty in her eyes that immediately made me believe her. Something told me there was more to it than she was letting on.

"Why?" I probed, taking every opportunity to hear her speak while I could. She was so mercurial, I had no idea if she would revert back to her usual manner, this time tomorrow. I didn't know what I would do if I was deprived of this again.

Jamie took a deep breath before answering me. "Can I tell you something?"

"Anything," I nodded quickly.

"My..." she tapered off, then looked up at me. She looked so conflicted as her dark eyes wandered from me then down to the ground. Her lip quirked as if she wanted to go on with it, but she hesitated yet again. Her internal struggle was presented clearly in her features. I waited patiently as Jamie's lips parted once more. I watched sympathetically as she pursed her lips, then looked up at the clear sky overhead. The sky seemingly posed as a mockery of her state, because even I could gauge the cloudiness in her mind, and she hadn't said a word. She then drew in another deep breath to muster up the strength to continue. "My brother died last summer."

I didn't know what I was expecting to hear, but certainly not that. My smile faltered slightly. I hardly knew how to respond. "Oh, I'm sorry..." I said quietly, and it was all I could manage to say.

"It's okay... It's not your fault. It's mine. And – Honestly, I have no idea why I just told you that, but I felt like I had to get it off of my chest. Ever since then, I've just–" Jamie started to explain, but I had to interrupt her.

"It's not your fault, Jamie," I said imperatively. My brow furrowed as I tried to make her grasp my seriousness about that. Her confession hit me hard, but I couldn't let her blame herself for that tragedy.

"Yes it was," she stated resolutely. For a moment, she was devoid of emotion. There was a blank expression on her face after disagreeing with me. I would've given anything to know what had gone through her mind at that disassociated moment. Her eyes were trained on nothing at all. And suddenly, I saw her getting teary–eyed. Her usually dark brown eyes were almost obsidian now, and they possessed so much sadness as I watched them gloss over. My joviality completely faded, crushed by the overwhelming desire to console her. But I had no idea how.

"It wasn't... You can't blame yourself for something like that... Don't–" I assured her, but this time she was the one to interrupt me.

"Yes it was, Anna. It's all my fault," Jamie repeated staunchly, and her voice cracked. I'd just gotten the privilege, and it seemed that I'd heard everything on the spectrum within those few minutes. "I should've just given him the money... Then it wouldn't have happened..." she continued, and the second that tear rolled down her cheek, I pulled her into my arms without any hesitance.

I'd never been good with death, and I'd never known what to say to those who had lost someone. Now was no different, but I felt compelled to try. Seeing my mystery girl cry was heartbreaking enough, but the story behind her tears was threatening to choke me up as well. Our atmosphere had shifted so suddenly, I was blindsided by where our conversation had gone. Nevertheless, we couldn't both be crying now. I felt that it was my duty to stay strong for her, because it was clear that no one else had been.

Jamie graciously seized my torso and buried her face into my shoulder. Her arms were wrapped securely around me, and I felt like I was keeping her safe. She was clutching onto me for dear life. As I sat there, steeling myself for her after she'd essentially collapsed into me, I felt like Jamie's rock. I felt as if I was the only one willing to be there for her. In a split second, I'd taken on the responsibility with no questions asked. I could tell that she rarely allowed this level of vulnerability and raw emotion to surface. So, I savored this moment.

It ended all too soon when she gingerly pulled away from me. "Sorry..." she mumbled an unnecessary apology as she ran her hands over her puffy features.

"Don't apologize, Jamie. You're entitled to your emotions. Let it out. I'm here for you, if you want me to be," I offered with glossy eyes. This was not the first conversation I expected to have with her. I thought it would be more of me marveling at her voice and her laughing at me, like we had been. But suddenly, that was over and I was holding her. I could hardly keep up. But I felt like I had to, for her.

"I'm a fucking mess," she sobbed quietly.

"No, you're not," I implored.

"I am. You can't change my mind, Al," Jamie shook her head and avoided my gaze.

"Al?" I questioned with an amused smile.

She slowly peeked up at me, then away from me sheepishly – as if she'd let it slip. "I– Um– I gave you a nickname. But – But I can just call you Anna... If you want..." she elaborated, and her voice was laced with insecurity.

It baffled me how someone with so much to offer to the world could be plagued with so many insecurities. Jamie radiated beauty, and I never saw anything less. My opinions didn't matter if she never saw it, herself.

"No, I love it," I reassured her with a warm smile. It was then that I found a way to distract her from dwelling on the accident.

"You do?" she questioned with a ghost of a smile. "I've just been saying it to myself... I didn't mean to actually call you that."

"Of course," I nodded and encouraged a wider smile with one of my own.

She finally smiled a smile that reached her eyes. Although they were slightly puffy, her eyes were shining. They contained a certain lumière that only her smile could match. She was so undeniably beautiful, my heart ached at the sight of her. Kissing her crossed my mind, but I ignored that desire. I longed to kiss her, but I knew I couldn't for fear of destroying what little bond we had. It was inappropriate and misplaced, anyhow. Now was not the time, anyway.

"Okay," Jamie breathed, and her relief was quite obvious.

"When did you come up with that?" I questioned with a curious smirk.

"A few weeks ago," she shrugged.

"Tell me about that," I said in an attempt to steer the conversation away from her source of sadness. "Where did that come from?"

"One day, I saw you before you looked up. It was a few days after you'd told me your name, and I wrote mine on that dollar. You were reading something, but I never caught the name of the book. When I tried to see it, all I could see was '*AL*' written on the side. I knew they had to be your initials, but instead of saying A-L, I just kind of started to pronounce it as a word," Jamie divulged softly as she distracted herself from me by picking at her jeans.

"I would've never guessed you were calling me by my initials, just now," I commented and let a soft giggle escape. I was so endeared with her aura in telling me this supposed secret of hers.

"I guess it's dumb that I was pronouncing it like that," she shrugged and continued her fascination in the fabric of her pants. "I'll probably call you A-L, then."

"You can call me whatever you want," I allowed her room to choose. I tried to pass this conversation off as trivial, but I was so happy that she'd deemed me worthy enough for a nickname of any sort. "As long as I get to hear you speak," I tacked on playfully, although I was serious.

"A-L, it is," Jamie decided. "I really remember that day. That was the day I really started to notice you."

"Really?" I marveled at her. She noticed me?

"Yeah. After you noticed me, I noticed you. I mean, I don't usually pay attention to a lot... I don't pay attention to people, much. But you were different, and you caught my attention, I guess. It began that day you actually started talking to me past just ringing me up... How you told me your name and everything. And the next few days after that, I just paid more attention. And when I came up with your nickname, I walked in and there you were," Jamie grinned indistinctly as she reminisced, and I couldn't believe that a memory of *me* had put that subtle smile on her face. "You were sitting with your chin in the palm of your hand and you were turning the page with the other. I thought you were beautiful. I remember that, clearly. And I just remember thinking to myself, *Look at my little Al...* And after that, it just kinda stuck, I guess. I don't know..." Jamie shrugged. "I've been calling you that in my head now for a while. But I think I like A-L better. Makes more sense to me, now that I think about it."

"That's cute," I smiled calmly, despite the fact that my heart was nearly beating out of my chest. I idly wondered if she was aware of my impending heart attack. Learning of her keen observation made me want to melt. That, along with the nature of her explanation. *She thinks I'm beautiful? My Al?*

I found that conversations with Jamie were ever–changing. One topic didn't last for long. By the time I'd grasped what we were talking about, the discussion had shifted to something entirely different. Not even five minutes ago, she was crying about the death of her brother, but now she was smiling and talking about nicknames. I embraced the new direction.

I just stared at her in wonder. I wondered how in what little time I'd known her, and even lesser time of *actually* talking to her, that she'd become so important to me. And how her presence seemed to make everything alright, even if just for a little while. I smiled at her in appreciation for being an odd factor in my life that brought me joy without fail. Even when she was crying, she made me happy. And she was staring back at me, reciprocating my smile with an adoration I couldn't place. Why she would be looking at *me* like that, I didn't know. But we just stared at each other and held each other's gaze for an intense moment.

"You are my favorite part of the day," Jamie informed me, and I felt my heart surge again. She seemed to have been reading my mind, and I gaped at her. "But then I go home and everything is fucked up again..." she added, and I felt my heart break in the same instance.

Her perception of herself upset me more than it probably should have. I racked my brain to think of something to say, and I thought of the one thing I'd always relied on when I was beside myself. I hoped that sharing it would ease some of her strife. Or perhaps make her a little more optimistic than she was making herself out to be. I wanted to help that.

"A few days ago, I was thinking about some things... And I realized that the saying 'there's always a rainbow after the rain' isn't entirely true. Because that day I was sad, and it was raining... But there was no rainbow afterwards. There *was* a sunset, though. And it was so, *so* damn beautiful. So, I don't know... I just feel like you should keep in mind that your sunset is coming. Sunsets are inevitable. Your happiness will come in due time, Jamie. Trust me," I shared openly.

An air of silence followed my story. I felt like Jamie was taking my words into consideration, because she looked incredibly thoughtful. She mused for a minute, then broke the silence.

"I think you're my sunset," Jamie said after a while. And with that, she stood up and collected her things. "I have to go. I'll see you tomorrow, Anna," she promised as she went in to hug me once more.

As I reciprocated her hug, my mind was reeling. *I'm her sunset? She's my sunset, too. She's been my sunset for quite some time now. But she doesn't mean it the same way I do... She couldn't. What does she mean, anyway? Do I simply just make her happy? Do I provide some relief in her day? Or was there a hidden message in that? Am I looking too deeply into this?*

I assumed the latter as I watched Jamie saunter away from the bench. And even from behind, she was so beautiful. I sighed despite myself, but it ended in a grimace. Those feelings were inappropriate. I wasn't supposed to be feeling that way. Jamie was finally becoming my friend. I refused to ruin it by developing unrequited feelings.

It was hard to remind myself that I wasn't supposed to be falling for this girl. However, when she said things like that to me, how could I not? She made it impossible not to fall, and I was making it impossible for her to catch me. My brain wouldn't allow the thought that she could possibly feel the same way. And I promised myself that I wouldn't set myself up to be heartbroken when my suspicions were confirmed.

Anna

"Hi Jamie," I greeted her as soon as the kinky–haired girl entered the shop. She simply waved, and my smile fell. I feared that yesterday was the last I'd heard of her voice.

She crossed the store and came up to my counter with a bright smile. "How are you?"

I couldn't help my sigh of relief. "I'm great... *Now*," I smiled as I raised my eyebrows.

"Why *now*?" she asked cheekily as she leaned over the counter on her forearms.

"No reason," I smirked and excused myself from my position behind the counter. I sauntered around it and came to a stop in front of her. "What are you looking for today?"

"You," she said simply.

"Me?" I squeaked in surprise, having fully expected to hear a certain genre or artist, or something related to music. That was an awfully pleasant turn of events.

"Yes, you. And it looks like I've found you," she kept up that adorable smile of hers.

"Why me?" I asked as I tried to ignore the raging butterflies.

"I want to talk to you," she beamed, and her expression was so infectious. I couldn't help mirroring her countenance.

"Okay, about what?" I smiled as well.

"Follow me," Jamie instructed softly as she slipped her hand into mine, leading me out of the door.

"Where are we going?" I questioned.

"You'll see," she answered evasively, but the smile that followed was enough to make me trust her. Despite my apprehension, I knew damn well that I would've followed her anyway.

I informed Cassie in haste about our apparent plans, and she shooed me off with a sly smirk. I didn't pay her antics any attention and I hoped Jamie hadn't, either. We walked down the street hand in hand, and it had been such a natural occurrence. Once again, her fingers were laced with mine and they held on so tightly. I thoroughly enjoyed our contact as she led me towards wherever. I didn't know when, nor why, the atmosphere between us changed, but it definitely had. I felt that yesterday was the beginning of a very close connection between us. Even before then, it was there without words. It was hidden in the silence.

But I couldn't let myself to get too attached to her. I had to keep my distance in order to keep those disobedient feelings at bay. With that in mind, I subtly removed my hand from her affectionate grasp. She gave me a funny look, but said nothing. I thought it strange that I'd actually preferred that.

We approached the entrance of a small park nearby, and I turned to her. "We're going to the park?"

"Mhm," she nodded as she kept her gaze in front.

Together, we walked along the now grassy terrain. We scaled a hill and crossed a small bridge before we ended up in a secluded area I'd never seen. I usually never ventured out this far on my own. I was always only interested in the swings anyway.

Jamie located a bench that didn't seem fit for use. It was old and wooden with black embroidering on the back. She took a seat and it creaked, but she gestured for me to sit next to her anyway. I complied tentatively and she faced me with a slight grin.

"Why are we here?" I questioned after a few minutes of silently taking in the scenery.

"I love this spot. It's so *away*, you know? It's just me and you," she smiled, and my heartbeat increased. She was grinning so broadly, I couldn't help but reciprocate. Her hand inched closer to mine, and soon it was in her hold again. This time, I didn't dare move it.

"Yeah... It's pretty quiet," I noted as I grew nervous. Being here with so little to distract myself from her threatened to expose me. In the middle of this park, sitting with her on yet another bench, I found myself questioning just how this had come to be.

"It's the perfect spot to think or to clear your mind," Jamie supplied as her thumb idly brushed over my skin. She focused down at our intertwined hands and I stole a glimpse at her.

"I could use some serenity," I mused as I gazed down at our embrace. Her hand was so soft as it moulded around mine.

"We all could," Jamie seconded thoughtfully. "Anything on your mind, A-L?"

"Nothing in particular," I fibbed, because she was really all that ever occupied my thoughts these days. "What about you?"

"There's always something on mine," Jamie said and turned to me. "Must be nice to have a clear head."

"You must come here a lot, then," I inferred and my eyes drifted back up to meet those compelling brown ones. I found it strange how I was also an owner of brown eyes, yet I was so drawn to Jamie's.

"Yeah, we used to come here all the time. Some days after leaving the store, we would stop by just to sit a while," Jamie elaborated slightly.

"We?" I repeated with such curiosity, I was sure Jamie picked up on it. Having verbal conversations with her was still such a new concept to grasp. I was still so thrilled to hear her voice. I'd hardly gotten used to it.

"Oh, Corey used to love it here too," she shrugged in a reminiscent daze.

"Corey..?" I trailed, unsure of who we were talking about.

"My brother," she answered distantly. "This was our secret spot. We came here to get away, since no one really knows it even exists," she elaborated.

I knew I'd asked, but I instantly wished I hadn't. I suddenly felt intrusive for being here. The fact that she'd taken me to her and her brother's secret spot was endearing, however. It spoke volumes to me.

"Oh," I replied dumbly. "Well, thank you for bringing me here. It's beautiful."

"Not the only beautiful thing here," Jamie said so quietly, I hardly made note of it. When I did, I couldn't contain my smile. I felt the need to change the subject again, because this was nearing dangerous territory.

"Am I the only one you talk to?" I inquired softly.

"Yes ma'am," she nodded.

"Really?" I gasped.

"Yeah..." she affirmed again.

"How long have you been mute?" I asked as I turned to face her. I was finally getting down to what I really wanted to know, what she'd evaded on the notepad.

She shrugged. "A while. There's no reason to talk to anyone else."

Anyone else. I repeated internally. *She wants to talk to me, and me alone. She doesn't want to talk to anyone else...* I mused as a goofy grin spread across my face.

"Oh," I settled on saying. I didn't want to disclose how happy that little comment made me. I hoped I was successfully remaining passive, despite my goofy smile. "So, Corey loved it here?"

Jamie shifted uncomfortably at my mention of him. It dawned on me that this girl had been carrying this burden on her shoulders for quite some time now. She'd been letting it weigh her down, preventing her from living life to the fullest. She'd been blinded by his death, so that she could no longer see the beauty of this world. I wanted to open her eyes.

"Yeah. We used to sit here and just talk about life... Kinda like I want to do with you today," Jamie smiled and tried to steer the conversation in another direction.

I gladly let her. I didn't want her to be upset again. It occurred to me that my probing about the silence she'd been living in all stemmed from her brother, and to best avoid another breakdown like before, it was probably best to stop asking so many questions relating to it. I admired Jamie for not telling me to *shut up*, already. She always answered me, regardless of how much pain it probably caused her. I told myself to put a cap on it, but I was unknowingly going to force her down the same road anyway.

"With me, huh?" I repeated and felt my cheeks heating up.

"With you," she affirmed. Her hold on my hand tightened slightly, and she ran her thumb over the back of my hand.

"Can I ask you something?" I questioned wantonly. "About, life."

"Of course," she smiled encouragingly.

"Well, two things..." I added.

"Ask them both," she chuckled.

"I feel like I ask too many questions..." I realized as I blushed a little, acknowledging my obsession.

"I love questions," she responded encouragingly. "Well, when they're coming from you. I promise you, I don't mind answering."

"Okay, the first one is: why do you buy an album every day? And the second one is: why did you say I was your sunset?" I asked softly. Both inquiries had been lingering at the back of my mind all day. The first, more so than the second.

Jamie laughed uncomfortably. "They kind of lead into each other... It's funny that you asked it that way..."

"Yeah?" I raised my eyebrows.

"Yeah," she nodded. "The first one has a backstory... And I'm not too eager to tell it... But I feel safe with you. And I trust you. So... I'll tell you," she sighed.

"You don't have to..." I trailed calmly, although my heart was beating faster from her admissions. *She feels safe with me. And she trusts me. That means more to me than she'll ever know.*

"I need to. I haven't really told anyone this in it's entirety..." she insisted. "And I mean – Brace yourself. It's kind of a lot to handle... It's um– It's kind of intense, I guess... But– But I'll tell you, anyway."

"Well, I don't want you to feel like I'm forcing you. You don't have to answer that if it's too much. But I'm all ears if you insist," I offered an understanding smile.

"I buy them for my brother," she started, and it instantly roused questions just like before. But I kept quiet until she finished. "We were outside of the music shop... The one you work at – You know. He always just liked to go. He was really into music. I don't know where he picked it up, but he suddenly became really obsessed with vinyl and CDs – he was especially into CDs... I was letting him use my old CD player that I used to have. He would listen to my music, and then he started wanting his own CDs to listen to because I'd basically given him my CD player by then. So, Small Wonder would be the perfect place for him, you know? But he never really bought anything..." she trailed.

Jamie was staring blankly ahead. Her gaze was focused on nothing in particular. She looked so distant, as if she would break at any given moment. I rubbed my thumb across the back of her hand soothingly, just like she'd done to me. I was silently encouraging her to go on, and she complied.

"But one day, he wanted to. He didn't have enough. He asked me for some extra cash to help him out, and I told him no. I had the money, Anna. More than enough, but I– I told him no..." she said shakily. I saw the tears forming in her eyes, and I felt my own eyes water. "We fought about it... I can't even believe how much of a bitch I was about it... I was being so inconsiderate and so mean... It cost eleven fucking dollars, Anna. I had hundreds on my card, and I wouldn't give it to him. I told him to go to the bakery instead – the same one you went to. I said just get whatever you can... And he didn't want me to go with him like I usually would have, because he was mad at me. And– And I didn't care, so I just said okay..." she continued painfully. One tear had fallen, but I quickly wiped it.

"I should've gone with him. I–I should've gone... And then it would've been me. That drunk driver would've hit me. Corey didn't deserve that..." she sobbed openly. "I do."

It was clear that she blamed herself for the accident. And that was all it was, it was an accident. I desperately wished she could see that. It pained me to see her so distraught and broken over something that was beyond her control like this.

"Don't say that," I said hoarsely. I knew my voice lacked the confidence and reassurance Jamie needed. I was on the brink of tears, myself.

"He was listening to his music... He had his headphones in and... He– He didn't hear it. He didn't hear the sirens. He didn't hear the car coming," she gasped. "And then it was too late..."

My heart ached as I listened to her recount this tragic story. In that moment, I could fully grasp how traumatizing that must've been. Her elective mutism was blatantly justifiable.

I couldn't imagine being in her position, and my little sister was the one that had died. I didn't want her to blame herself, but I could understand her point of view. It probably felt like it *was* her fault, when in reality it was just an accident. If it were my supposed sister's accident, I would probably react the same way. As an only child, I had no real way of relating. But I could imagine. Jamie obviously shared that kind of bond with her late brother.

I hadn't realized I was lost in my musings until Jamie started to apologize. "I'm sorry. That was just really intense for me... I didn't mean to get so emotional on you..."

"You are entitled to your emotions," I said simply. I felt guilty for not responding. I didn't want her to worry about what I was thinking. In my eyes, she could do no wrong.

"Thank you," Jamie said graciously. She then used both hands to wipe her face.

She drew in a deep breath to compose herself. "And... To answer the second part of your question... I feel like some things are taken away from you for a reason. I'm starting to think that all of this shit has happened to me just so we could cross paths. It happened so I could meet someone like you," she said genuinely. "To bring me out of it."

I felt like my heart would explode. Her admission caused so many unwanted feelings. I didn't need this from someone who was supposed to be my friend. She was making it impossible to *not* fall for her. And she wasn't finished.

"I... I haven't been happy since the accident. But I'm happy when I'm with you, Anna. I'm *happy* – And its *real*. You're bringing me out of it in your own way. I just, I don't know. I'm really glad I met you," she expressed honestly.

"Jamie..." I trailed as I stared at my lap. Her words elicited so many things within me, I didn't know which emotion to act on. I felt heavy with the realization that I'd apparently played such an important role in her life. She'd given me the responsibility of bringing her out of it, and now I felt like it was my duty. And I made her happy? I wanted to keep that smile on her face forever.

"I'm serious," she insisted.

"I'm glad I met you, too. I mean, *of course* I am. You give me something to look forward to, every single day. I'm happiest with you," I returned with the same amount of sincerity. "You said it yesterday and all, but really, you're *my* favorite part of the day, too."

After a few seconds of staring down, I built up the courage to meet her eyes. That sepia abyss was full of promise. She really meant what she'd said, and it was so obvious now that I looked at her. We were staring, and there was this new air between us – an air of mutual attraction. As cliché as it might've been, I got lost. My mind went blank, and I was spurred on by what my heart wanted. I felt myself indistinctly leaning in, uncertainly, and Jamie wasn't moving away. In fact, she didn't seem to be averse to it at all.

As I did, I thought about it. My feelings for her were starting to scare me. She made me feel things I'd never felt before. It had been solidified as a crush already. There was no doubt that I liked Jamie – that I *really* liked Jamie. This was deeply–rooted. There weren't simple butterflies in my stomach, it was a tidal wave of emotions I wasn't prepared to deal with. I felt tsunamis crashing against my ribcage when she walked in. Her touch didn't just make me blush, it set my skin ablaze and ignited every fiber of my being. I felt a lot for my mystery girl. It was increasing exponentially by the day. The next thought that crossed my mind made me pause. We weren't nearly there yet, but could I love a girl that was this damaged?

Of course, I could. And it terrified me.

Jamie and I were much too close, now. We had both angled our bodies in preparation for – whatever. Had we been about to kiss? Was she about to allow that? Had she considered it? My heart lurched uncomfortably at the thought of it. I wasn't prepared. A kiss now still seemed inappropriate, although Jamie seemed to be receptive to the idea. I straightened up and averted my gaze, and I saw Jamie do the same out of my peripheral vision. Then, there was regret. Whatever had been about to happen, sure wasn't going to happen now.

Neither of us said a word about it. Suddenly, the silence was unbearable. For two individuals that were still learning how to overcome that, I felt that we'd both forgotten how. I couldn't stand to be in such an awkward predicament any longer. "Uh– I should probably – I have to go."

"Anna–" Jamie started. She looked so worried, but I couldn't be there any longer.

"No, sorry. I have to um– Babysit!" I lied, and I didn't like my dishonesty with her, but I felt that it was necessary. "I just remembered, sorry. I'll see you tomorrow, Jamie. Goodnight," I excused myself as I quickly scrambled back the way I'd come.

I knew exactly what I'd done, and I wasn't going to try to play coy. I knew that I was nearly about to kiss her, then chickened out. But she hadn't moved.

If she didn't like me, she would've moved... Right? She would've said "What the hell are you doing, Anna?", just like the rational part of my brain was screaming. But she didn't move... I mused as I frantically tore away from the bench. That gave me little hope for tomorrow, and I briskly walked home. I had to get away from her.

Jamie

When Anna left yesterday, everything came crashing down. I couldn't stop her from fleeing, from running away from me. There was no argument about whether she'd had to babysit or not, it was obviously a poor excuse. It was unlikely, but perhaps I'd come on too strong. Perhaps I'd made her uncomfortable. Perhaps I'd been misreading her advances all along. I'd gotten it all wrong, and I felt awful.

I felt like I'd ruined yet another good thing in my life. And I figured that was why good things didn't happen to me. I always ruin it. That had been my story since I ended Corey's life: mine was to be ruined from then on. I'd always known there was a limit on my time with Anna. Everything that was worthwhile was temporary for me. I just didn't see it going up in flames so suddenly like that. One minute, we were being honest and vulnerable, and the next, she couldn't get away from me fast enough.

Then, it dawned on me that maybe it wasn't my forward approach. It could've been what I'd told her about Corey. She was the first and only one, and maybe that was a mistake. I didn't know why I trusted her. I didn't know why I thought she would be different, or that she would understand. She seemed receptive, but she was probably just pretending for my sake. At first – When I began. There was silence after I'd finished. Now that I considered it, she was probably reassessing me. She was probably regretting her pursuit. She was probably dumbstruck with my reality. She probably wanted no part of it.

Having that conversation come after oversharing about Corey was a poor decision on my part. I'd probably overwhelmed the poor girl with all of that emotion. Anna had probably made up her mind about me. She probably realized that I was responsible for Corey's death. She was probably disgusted with me. A reaction like that was the very reason I'd kept it to myself. Much like his premature one, I decided that I would carry this secret to my grave.

I had half a mind to not even show up to the music store, but I couldn't stand to miss her. I also couldn't stand the pang of guilt I felt for not going to get Corey's album. All it took was reminding myself that my selfishness was the reason that he'd died to change my mind. When I pushed through the door, she almost looked relieved to see me. I smiled slightly in an odd form of greeting. She offered me a shy smile as I approached the counter. I already felt estranged.

"Hi, Jamie," she said meekly.

"Hi. How was babysitting?" I questioned condescendingly. I crossed my arms insecurely as I waited for her response.

"What?" she questioned, then realized my reference. It was clear that she'd lied yesterday and had done no such thing. "Oh, it was fine... Are you looking for anything in particular?

We just got some new shipments–" she tried, but I wasn't going to play along today.

"I thought I'd scared you away," I admitted, and her eyebrows raised in surprise at my candor. I was surprised, too.

"You did, a little," she said, and my heart dropped. "But – But not for the reasons you think..."

"If it wasn't what I told you about Corey... What was it, then?" I wondered aloud, and Anna was avoiding my gaze. I was specific because she'd considered what was already on my mind. Might as well address it head–on.

"Can we go to the park again?" she asked, evading my question.

"Um, sure... Yeah, we can go..." I agreed hesitantly. I figured she sought for privacy to let me down. Anna gave me a tight–lipped smile and backed away from the counter. I tried to maintain a straight face and remain optimistic. I didn't know where this was headed, but I couldn't go into it with any negative assumptions.

"Let me just tell Cassie I'm going on my break now," she excused herself to the back room. With what little knowledge I had to go off of, I gathered that it had more to do with Corey and less to do with the feelings we both so clearly experienced. It was a bittersweet revelation. I had her ambiguous explanation looming over my head, but it didn't decrease my small smile at what was present now.

"What?" she questioned with a slow smile when she returned. My arms were crossed and I was smiling, as small as it may have been. She noticed it and questioned it.

"Nothing, I just..." I laughed to myself and held my arms closer against my chest. "Nothing."

"Tell me?" she encouraged me softly.

"I know you've been putting off going on your breaks just to hang out with me," I admitted. I wouldn't confront her about her feelings or expose my own, unnecessarily. That was a safe, flirty observation.

"Uh... No I don't," she stuttered and met my eyes challengingly. She was staring at me with an open–mouthed smile as she tried her hand at denying it. She was adorable. "I have no idea what you're talking about."

"You totally do. I figured that out a while ago. You're so cute, A-L," I laughed in the warm atmosphere we shared. I wanted to experience the full benefits of this air, because I had the horrible feeling that it was going to be taken away from me with whatever she had to say once we got to the park.

Realizing that she'd been caught, her cheeks reddened. I'd never truly seen someone blush before. It was precious. "Whatever. You're not special or anything," she joked. "You just happen to arrive when I decide to go on my break. How do I know you're not plotting *your* visits based on when *I* have my breaks, hmm?"

The way she made light of it and brushed it off with humor made me giggle even more. "Oh, sure. You caught me."

Anna swatted my shoulder and grasped my arm sheepishly. "Come on..."

I let her lead me out of the doors and back towards the park. When we reached the territory that was still unfamiliar to her, she faced me. "Which way is it from here?"

"This way," I answered as I slipped my hand into hers. I caught her smiling to herself from the corner of my eye, but I didn't say anything. But I resonated with her.

"So, benches are kind of our thing? Aren't they?" she inferred as we took a seat.

"Perhaps," I nodded.

"Before you brought me here, we used to sit on the bench outside of the store. I think they are," Anna reasoned and I smiled at her. I sensed her need for distraction, and I was willing to let her.

"In that case, they are. This is our thing," I declared with a broad smile.

"Good," she grinned as well. She turned to face me, and then we were both smiling at each other. As usual. Her presence alone could bring a smile to my face, but when I got to witness hers, it was impossible to keep mine off. Her simplistic beauty baffled me, even more so when she was smiling at me this way.

"You are so beautiful," I breathed. I spoke my inner thoughts aloud, but it didn't faze me. The entire world knew that Anna was beautiful. It was no secret. I figured I should let her know as well – in addition to posing a distraction.

"Oh, thank you..." she mumbled as she broke eye contact. Her silent disagreement was clear on her face. I saw it in the subtle eyebrow raises and the slight shrug of her shoulders. She had no need to be humbled. And it wasn't humility. It disheartened me that she got so insecure when she was easily the most beautiful girl, inside and out, that I'd ever met.

"I mean it. You're my beautiful little sunset," I expressed honestly as my smile returned. Flattery earned me a shy grin and delayed her news.

"Jamie," Anna breathed. She seemed overwhelmed again. With pursed lips, her brow furrowed and she looked as if she was in deep thought. Her eyes darted to me, then back down to her lap. She twiddled her thumbs wantonly and bit her lip. I didn't know what was going on, but I wanted to relieve her of whatever it was. To hell with distraction.

"Yes? What? What is it?" I prompted softly.

"I wanted to come here for a reason," she disclosed.

"Which would be..." I trailed guardedly, unsure of where this conversation was headed.

"You know how I kind of ran away yesterday... And then today when you said you thought you'd scared me away...?" she started in a tone laced with trepidation.

"Yeah?" I answered, dreading how she would connect the two.

"Well... You make me nervous. But it's the good kind of nervous. Not like *I'm gonna throw up* type of nervous..." she attempted to explain, and I kinked an eyebrow in amusement. "It's like... Butterflies and blushing and confusion and all of this weird stuff I'm not used to..." she continued and was so flustered.

I vaguely had a sense of what she was hinting at. It didn't seem to confirm either of my fears at all. In fact, it seemed to oppose my impression. But I didn't want to get my hopes up. Wishful thinking had never done me any good in the past. So, I pushed that option to the back of my mind and heard her out.

"I don't know why it happens... Well – Yeah, I do. You're so pretty and kind of intimidating... From your looks, not your personality. Like – You're a sweetheart, but you just look so... You're pretty – Really pretty... With your pretty hair and your pretty eyes... And I didn't even really think that brown eyes were all that pretty, before you. But yours are pretty. And it makes me nervous. You love to look directly into my eyes – like – like you are right now..." Anna addressed my focus and I looked away to make it easier on her. "And I can't handle it.

I get all antsy when you look at me and my heart beats faster and my palms get all gross and sweaty..." Anna kept rambling, and I was grinning so hard.

"And... It's been happening for the longest time, but it wasn't always this bad. It got worse when I started talking to you. Well, when *you* started talking to *me*. When I heard your voice, it just... It all became too much. And then hearing your voice on top of the things you were saying to me... It's a lot to process... And it makes me feel all of these feelings I'm not familiar with," she sighed. She was refusing to make eye contact with me, and I thought it was adorable. She was clearly flustered by her confessions, but I was endeared and completely smitten.

"I don't want you to be weirded out or anything but... I think I like you, Jamie. Like, *like–like*. Like... I *really*, kind of, *like* you... A lot," she finally announced, then didn't give me the chance to respond before she inferred my perception of it. "And – I know what you're thinking. It's weird to me, too... But I don't want things to change. I don't want you to feel awkward or to treat me any differently because of this. I'm sure these feelings will go away soon, but–" she rambled, and I couldn't endure it any longer. I had the insatiable urge to kiss her, so I did.

I interrupted Anna in the best way. The second our lips connected, she melted into me. Her hand lifted to cup my cheek as she leaned into me. My eyes were initially closed, but when they opened and I saw how close she was, I couldn't help my stupid smile. Although it only lasted a few mere seconds, I'd never been more placated in my life. Nor as content.

Anna exhaled sharply when we parted and she looked dazed. Her lips were slightly swollen, and I smirked at the realization that it was my fault. I'd just claimed this girl. She was already mine, whether she knew it or not. And I was all hers.

"You kissed me," Anna noted aloud, almost in disbelief.

"Yes, thank you Captain Obvious," I laughed. She had a knack for verbalizing things that shocked her. She'd done the same when I spoke to her for the first time. It was one of the cuter observations I'd made of her.

"Sorry..." she trailed, but a smile soon overtook her features and she turned her head away.

"It was mutual, you know," I informed her. Finally, it felt that I was somewhat at ease with her. I was no longer walking on eggshells. Anna wasn't either.

"It was?" Anna asked obliviously.

"Everything you said," I elaborated. "I feel the same way. And I thought you'd caught on, but I guess not."

"*You did*?" she questioned incredulously.

"Yes. I almost kissed you yesterday, but then you freaked out on me..." I playfully chastised her. I thought she was aware of my attraction, just like I was aware of hers. I'd given her intuition a little too much credit.

"I'm sorry. I thought it was only one–sided..." she apologized. "I knew that you knew that I wanted to kiss you... And I was gonna, but I just got so scared. Somehow, I made myself think that I was in it all by myself. And I mean – No one ever likes me back. So, I just... Psyched myself out. And then I thought that maybe you wouldn't be comfortable with me just planting one on ya. I did a lot of thinking – too much, I guess."

"Don't," I warned. I took her hand into mine again and caressed her soft skin with my thumb in the same habit I'd been falling into. I liked my habit, and that it was ours. Her hand clutched mine, and I brought it to my lips gently. "It wasn't one–sided at all," I promised her.

"Really?" she asked meekly.

"Yeah," I nodded. "I thought this was one of those situations where we just both knew how we felt. I didn't think I'd need to ever come out and say that I liked you, or to hear that you liked me, too. I guess I thought that maybe we skipped that? Or something?"

"No, I don't take hints. You just told me that you liked me and part of me is still being dumb and wondering how you mean that," Anna joked – or at least I thought she was joking. "You have to tell me everything."

"I'm willing to do that," I granted. "By the way – spoiler alert – I have the biggest crush on you."

The beautiful smile I was awarded with made me smile in response. Anna leaned into me slightly and I brought my arms over her gently. I caressed her indistinctly as we sat on that bench in a reflective silence. We were both letting it marinate. I was enjoying having her in my arms.

"I guess part of me kinda knew you liked me back, a little. When I leaned in yesterday, you didn't move away or anything," Anna pointed out the very factor that should've been her green light. I couldn't imagine how she'd talked herself out of that one.

"Well, because I was hoping you'd kiss me. Because I wanted to," I nodded and giggled to myself.

"Why, though? I've never done anything to make you like me..." she trailed.

"Are you kidding? No one has ever paid as much attention to me as you do," I started off, although it didn't stem from vanity at all. It wasn't her attention that I liked.

"Well, you were so weird. But it was the good kind of weird that made me want to get to know you. Call me cliché, but I like what I can't have. I couldn't have conversations with you or hear your voice and it just made me so damn determined to get through to you," she explained. "I just wanted to figure you out, Jamie."

I laughed. "Yeah, I know. You wanted to get to know me. *Me*. Just Jamie. Not Jamie whose brother died... Not the story behind what I'd seen... Just... Me. And I loved that. I can tell that I matter to you..."

"You're special to me," Anna said with an adorable smile. She grazed her finger over my eyebrow in brushing my hair away from my face. I furthered her attempt by tucking it beneath my cap and I cuddled into her. After hearing her admission, I enveloped her in another full hug. My arms wrapped around her tiny torso and I buried my face into her shirt. Anna's arms felt like home to me. I was safe when I was here.

"Jamie?" Anna prompted.

I shifted to look up at her. "Yes?"

"Does... Does that mean we're like, a thing then?" she asked tentatively.

"What do you mean?" I questioned.

"Like... Are you my– um... My..." Anna trailed as she struggled to find the words. "I mean – I know it doesn't automatically mean anything just because we kissed and said all of that, but like–" she stopped herself. I smirked at her and sat up completely as I watched her fumble with her words. She was so riled up, it was incredibly adorable. Her cheeks were flushed once again as she tried to articulate her thoughts properly. "I want– If we could be like – Like – If you wanted – We could be–" she stuttered, and I just put her out of her misery.

"I'm yours. Whatever that means to you, yes. I'm yours," I promised her and meant it wholeheartedly. The smile that followed immediately after let me know that I'd made the right choice. We could formally ask and make it official later. But for now, this sufficed for both of us. We were sufficient for each other.

"You're mine?" she grinned. She seemed so elated by this information.

A huge smile graced my lips as well when she reiterated it. "Of course. I've always been yours, A-L."

"If you're mine... Does that mean I can kiss you?" Anna asked softly. She seemed so timid and unsure of herself, I just wanted to hug her. Anything she did would be okay with me.

"Hmm, I don't know..." I smirked as I came closer to her. I got impossibly close to her lips, to the point where they were almost touching. They weren't, and I was enjoying teasing her. "Does it?" I challenged. In our close proximity, her breath tickled my lips as she exhaled shakily. All she had to do was tilt her chin to connect them.

She got the hint and placed both hands on my cheeks as she tentatively pressed her lips to mine. I felt the corners of her mouth turn up into a smile as she rested her forehead against mine. We turned to face each other and engaged in a series of similar, chaste kisses that made my heart flutter. Nothing was official and we had no title, but this much was clear: Anna was mine and I was hers.

Anna

I loved being the daughter of such loving parents. And I loved being friends with such amazing people. I loved being an employee at Small Wonder. I loved being a temporary resident of Savannah and I loved being a part of the LGBT community. I loved being a lot of things, but being Jamie's was my favorite.

It was unclear what we were exactly, because we had never discussed it further. Essentially, labels were not important when she made me feel like her girlfriend. She treated me like I was. In the past week, she'd greeted me with kisses instead of silent waves. She'd never missed a chance to give me a compliment or to hold my hand. She hadn't been painfully closed off, the way she used to be. I'd been in a state of bliss all week. Before I was hers, I waited for her arrival every day. I still did now, but it was always much harder to wait. She was punctual every day, so I never had to miss her for too long.

"Hi, Jamie," I smiled broadly as I saw her open the door.

"Hey, babe," she greeted me, seconds before pecking my lips quickly. I felt my cheeks heat up the way they always did, and she brushed my cheekbone with her thumb. "You're so cute, A-L."

"So are you. Are you looking for anything in particular today?" I questioned.

"I've already found you. What else could I possibly need?" she countered sweetly.

"Corey's album," I said as I retrieved it from behind the counter. "You know how much it is," I chuckled as I scanned it.

Jamie paid and smirked at me when I placed it back in the register. "Let's go somewhere new today," she said when I met her eyes.

"Okay, where?" I asked as I leaned over the counter.

"I want you to come over," she clarified. "We haven't been to each others' houses yet and I'm tired of the bench."

"Oh," I nodded awkwardly. "Sure, when?"

"When you get off?" she suggested.

"I get off in an hour," I noted as I checked the clock. "Do you just wanna come back?"

"No, I'll stay. You're cute when you're working," she smirked.

"So, you're just going to watch me like a creeper?" I inferred with a laugh. "I'm warning you, there's not a whole lot to see..."

"There's nothing else I'd rather be doing," she smiled.

"Would you two lovebirds just get out of here already? Anna, you and Jamie are making me sick," Cassie teased us playfully as she appeared from the back.

"Are you sure?" I questioned, eager to get away with Jamie.

"You act like this place is ever busy, anyway. We never need more than one person working here at a time," Cassie laughed. "Go ahead. I can cover the register."

"Really? Oh my God, I love you," I said as I turned back to Jamie with a broad smile.

"Yeah, go ahead," she nodded with a knowing smirk.

I walked over to pull her into a gracious hug. When her arms wrapped around me, she leaned in to whisper in my ear. "She's good for you. Make your move," Cassie said before we pulled away.

I nodded and grabbed my jacket from the back of the chair. I didn't quite know what she meant by telling me to make my move. In a way, I already had. I was perfectly fine with being Jamie's without a title. It was in the back of my mind during the entire walk to Jamie's house.

"You actually live within walking distance," I noted as the ten–minute walk led us to a modest home. Hand in hand with Jamie, we walked along the sidewalk and then cut through a pass in the woods. Once we'd gotten to the other side, we were in the middle of a neighborhood. I figured Jamie had created that trail herself from that daily trek.

"Yeah, and it's a good thing, too, because I don't drive," she chuckled and gestured to the house I assumed was hers. "I couldn't bring myself to learn after what happened."

"I don't drive either," I seconded meagerly as we ascended her concrete stairs. I stood to the side as Jamie rummaged for her keys, then pushed open the door. She escorted me inside with a hand on the small of my back.

Upon entering, I found that the Holden household was very warm and inviting. Pictures of Jamie, Corey, and another small child lined the walls, hallways, and mantelpiece. I didn't even know she had a sister. I briefly wondered if that was how she was treated ever since their brother's death. Were they both constantly ignored and disregarded? The thought alone made my heart ache.

"You have a sister?" I asked as I looked at the plethora of baby pictures.

"Yeah, her name is Sam. I've never told you about her before?" Jamie asked incredulously. I shook my head and her eyebrows furrowed. She seemed upset that we'd never spoken of this before. "Really? Never?" she pressed.

"No. I didn't know you had another sibling. I just thought it was you and Corey," I shrugged. "That's crazy. Is she here?"

"Well, yes I have a sister. Her name is Sam and she's four years younger than me," she added. "And I'm not sure, but I think she should be. You can meet her, if she is."

"She's pretty," I smiled as I gazed at the photos along the mantelpiece again. "You've got good genes," I added cheekily.

"So do you," she giggled. "But come on. Let's go up to my room," she suggested as she slipped her hand into mine. I quickly took in the rest of my surroundings as I followed her up to her room. They were obviously a family that loved their pictures. I was certain there was a picture present from every era of Jamie's adorable life. She was just as beautiful as a baby as she was now. I didn't have the time to scrutinize the photographs as I would've liked. We were zipping through her house, up the stairs, and down the hallway until we reached her room.

When I entered, my eyes were drawn to the shelf that was lined with books above her closet. That was probably where she housed the selections I always saw her reading on the bench, before everything. I turned to her with a knowing smile as I continued to look around. She had two beds, both equipped with white comforters. To the left hung a flat screen television in the corner, and a plastic storage drawer aligned on the wall. Her room was relatively small, but it would probably look a lot more spacious without the clutter.

"Your room is cool," I smiled as I took a tentative seat on her bed.

"It's not, you don't have to say anything," she laughed and cleared off some space on her bed by tossing things onto the other bed. "I share it with Sam, so," she shrugged.

"Well, *I* like it," I said pointedly as I removed my shoes. I took a seat next to her and sat here idly.

"Thanks, A-L," she smiled as she gave me an Eskimo kiss. Her nose was warm as it nuzzled over mine.

"You're welcome," I giggled as I sat cross–legged in front of her. She copied my stance and picked up my hands, filling the space between my fingers with her own. She played with my hands for a while, and I just gazed at her in adoration. Kind of dating Jamie was quickly becoming one of the best eras of my life.

But I longed to know her. I knew a significant amount of random things about her, but I wanted to know her inside and out. I wanted to know her passions and her fears, what songs make her dance and what movies make her cry, which prejudices make her angry and which books placate her. I wanted to know her embarrassing stories and her proudest moments, who she looked up to and her inspirations. I was desperate to find out her plans for the future and if the thought alone scared her like it did me, and if she had any odd phobias or collections, or which insecurities she thought plagued her body and if she'd ever had self image issues, or any mental health ailments I could assist her with at all. I wanted to know her story, not the story of her brother's death; I just wanted to know *her*.

When I came back from my musings, Jamie was staring at me. With a sliver of light shining through the window and bathing her caramel skin, her eyes were a stunning shade of brown. They were illuminated, ablaze. I wondered if her eyes reflected her mood. I wondered if she was as happy as I was in this moment. Before she started talking again, she was such a cynical being. I could tell that much from how she previously carried herself. I actually feared that she was depressed, but looking at her now, she seemed to be anything but. Perhaps she'd been putting on a rather believable façade, but we generally stayed away from those kinds of dark conversations. There was a notable difference, however. Her smile finally reached her eyes, and I loved that I could discern that change in her. The notion that I might've had something to do with that just about melted my heart. Her happiness was my happiness.

"What are you thinking about?" she asked intuitively as she brushed her thumb along the back of my hand.

"You," I answered simply.

"Yeah? Are they good thoughts?" Jamie questioned as she tilted her head slightly.

"They always are," I nodded. "I was just thinking about how much I wanted to know you," I disclosed quietly. It was kind of silly for me to have all of these supposed deep feelings when we didn't know much about one another at all.

"You want to know me?" she repeated. "You're getting to know me every day, love."

"Yeah, like I know a couple of random things, but I feel like I'm a long way from *knowing* you, if that makes sense," I shrugged and picked up her hand again.

"No, it makes perfect sense. I was thinking that the other day, too. And I mean, there's no formula for getting to know someone... You just have to start talking," she said after a thoughtful moment. I found it pretty ironic.

"Yeah. It's like you have to ask the right questions to produce those telling kind of answers," I agreed. "It just comes in time, I guess. But I'm really impatient all of a sudden."

"Well, we have all the time in the world right now, baby," she smiled, and her use of the name released a multitude of butterflies within me. "Let's get started. Ask me a question."

"Um–" I started, but Jamie spoke again before I could come up with my first one.

"But don't ask me anything basic, like my favorite color or food... Ask me a real question," she added.

"Why can't I ask you what your favorite color is?" I challenged.

"Because who gives a shit about someone's favorite color when you've got a whole mind to explore?" she countered. "I just think those types of questions are pointless. Nobody remembers half of that stuff anyway."

Her response made me smile. I agreed wholeheartedly, and her point of view was eye–opening. I probably had been about to ask her what her favorite color was, or something of the same strand, but I was glad she'd interrupted me. Nevertheless, I would've remembered her favorite color – had she told me. No detail about Jamie would ever be deemed insignificant.

"See, that's what I mean. I want to know stuff like that... And I didn't even have to ask you a question to get that. You've got a beautiful mind," I complimented her as I leaned in to peck her lips. I still found it surreal that I had the privilege.

"So do you, A-L. I can't wait to find out more about you. Go," she smiled.

"Hmm... Passions. Tell me about your passions," I decided to ask first. "What are you passionate about, Jamie?"

"Passions..." she repeated as she looked up at the ceiling, seemingly contemplating her answer. "Well, I guess I can start off with my main passions... I love to write. I love words and I just think the way they can be strung together sometimes is so beautiful – like, that's what I wanna be able to do. I wanna be like – a wordsmith. I want to make people fall in love with my words the way I'm always falling in love with someone else's. My goal with my writing is to make people feel – Feel, whatever. I don't have a preference, but I just want them to experience something, you know?"

"I love that so much," I marveled at her. "I love people that want to create. I love words, too. I love writing just as much as I love reading. Like, you know that feeling you get when you read a passage and it really just resonates with you? When a line just hits you – that's the best feeling."

"Yeah! I just love language and learning new words," Jamie nodded animatedly, and I adored her. "And I get really passionate about politics and world issues on a global context. I'm really in–tune with the news, or at least I try to be," she said, and I knew there was more she was willing to delve into with that, but she changed her mind. "And I'm pretty passionate about music. For the longest time, I wanted to be a singer, but I've read too much into it and I've literally seen how the industry chews people up and spits them out – so, I've let that go, for the most part. I still write my own songs a little bit, though. What I haven't let go of is that I just think it would be so dope to see people out there vibing to your creation. I don't know," she mentioned with a distant smile.

I opened my mouth to respond, but I suddenly sensed someone's presence in the doorway. When I turned to face it, my suspicions were confirmed. There in the threshold, with her mouth agape, stood an older woman that resembled Jamie.

"Jamie? I've almost forgotten what your voice sounds like," the woman I assumed to be her mother said with impenetrable eyes. I couldn't decipher what her tone was, exactly. "I haven't heard you speak so fluently in so long..."

Jamie paused and turned to her awkwardly. "Uh, hi."

"Hello..." she returned stiffly, then settled her gaze on me. "Who is your friend?"

"Anna... This is my mom, Margaret. Mom, this is Anna. My um – Anna," she reiterated with a goofy grin.

I smiled politely in response, although I was slightly disappointed. A part of me wanted her to introduce me as her girlfriend, but I knew I couldn't have expected that when neither of us had asked and it hadn't been discussed. Feeling like her girlfriend and being her girlfriend were two different things entirely. I waved at her mother regardless.

"Nice to meet you," Margaret said with a distracted smile, but she was staring so intently at Jamie. She'd mentioned me to be polite, but I could tell that I was the least of her concerns after the revelation of hearing her daughter speak.

Jamie's mother gazed at me quizzically, and I wished I could tell what she was thinking. Was it strange for Jamie to have people over? Did Jamie even have friends to invite over anymore? Did she not even speak at home? Was that an exaggeration on her mother's part? Had her entire life been put on hold, and eventually at a stand–still since the accident? Everything about their interaction was peculiar. They both seemed so estranged. I hoped all was well.

"You too, Mrs. Holden," I smiled back sympathetically as I recalled how I was the only person Jamie ever talked to openly. I realized that apparently, she'd meant that. I couldn't believe her own mother was also deprived of her voice. In the time we'd become friends, I'd nearly forgotten that she was mute ninety percent of the time we'd known each other. It made my heart ache that her own mother probably had to bear that same burden of not hearing her speak.

"Well... I'll leave you girls to it..." she said as she turned to leave. "And again, nice to meet you, Hannah."

"*Anna*," Jamie corrected her pointedly. I was just going to let her go on without correcting her, as I usually did.

"Jamie..." I admonished discreetly as I gave her mom an apologetic smile. "It's fine."

"Anna," Margaret corrected herself awkwardly before slipping out of view.

"Why did you do that?" I asked with a nervous laugh. I suddenly felt out of place. The tension between Jamie and Margaret was extremely palpable.

"Do what? Your name is Anna," she shrugged with a slight grimace. "It's simple enough and it deserves to be pronounced. I hate when people go without correcting people when they screw up their names. That's something that bothers me, since you want to get to know me. Acclimating bothers me so much, like, don't adjust for other people. They have the capacity to learn how to say your name right."

"I agree with you, but it just happens so much. Nowadays I just answer to whatever. Some days I'm Anna, some days I'm Hannah, some days I'm... *Annie*. Half the time when I tell them, they'll go right back to pronouncing it the way they want to. It just gets annoying. And you just don't try anymore after a while," I said with an air of resignation.

"Well then you shouldn't be surrounding yourself with those people. The least people can do is say your name right – at the *very* least. If they can't, they really don't deserve to interact with you at all, in my opinion," Jamie digressed as she looked back to the doorway.

"Well... In her defense, I'm sure she wasn't paying the most attention to my name..." I commented uncertainly. "If that's the first time she's heard you talk in a while..."

"She was being dramatic. I do talk to her. Most of the time, there's not a whole lot to say. That's what she meant by '*fluently*'," Jamie mumbled with agitation. "It's not a big deal. Back to the questions... Whose turn is it?"

"I'll go. Are you and your mom okay?" I asked intuitively, although I knew the probable answer. But I wanted to know why, because it seemed to be a lot deeper than her mother getting my name wrong. That was active displacement.

"We've definitely been on better terms, before," Jamie scoffed and cut her eyes towards the door again.

"Did something happen, babe?" I questioned softly.

"Really, she blames me for Corey's death," Jamie put it bluntly, looking away from me distractedly.

"What? But I thought you said no one really knew what happened?" I broached.

"She doesn't know *that*. She thinks it was my fault because everything is my fault," Jamie told me vaguely, and per usual, I had a plethora of questions.

"Oh," I mumbled as I decided not to ask them. Things were lighthearted, I didn't want to dampen our good mood. Much to my surprise, Jamie continued without my prompting.

"I'm the oldest, and I guess that means I'm the one that's always supposed to watch out for and take care of Corey and Sam. If they do anything wrong, it's my fault because I should've been there to discourage it. If they get hurt, it's my fault because I should've been there to protect them. I guess I'm just supposed to take care of myself and everyone around me. They were both my responsibility, but I wasn't anyone's. It's always been like that. And she's never *said* that she thinks it's my fault that Corey got hit, but she doesn't have to. I know that's what she's thinking every time she looks at me," Jamie bitterly explained to me and focused her attention on ripping out a string from her comforter.

"That's not your place, though," I argued on her behalf.

"Yeah, I know that. Try telling her that," Jamie muttered. "I've always tried to keep my distance from my mom because she always just makes me feel like absolute shit. The elective mutism thing I had going on was really easy to keep up because no one cares about me that much, anyway. The only time my mom said anything to me was to yell at me for something I had nothing to do with. And my dad tried to alleviate it, but he got distant after what happened, too. They care for me and all, but anything past what's necessary just seems really disingenuous."

"You do not deserve that," I said lowly, truly sympathetic for what she had to deal with on a daily basis. "What the hell..."

"The reason I'm that way towards her is because when we finally had that family conversation to come to terms with what happened, she turned it into an interrogation. She looked directly at me, Anna. And she didn't say anything, but she didn't have to. I knew exactly what she was thinking. *Where were you? How could you let him run into the street like that? Why didn't you do anything?* All of those fucking questions are there on her face, every time I look at her. It makes me sick. I will never forget the way she looked at me. And I can't forgive her for blaming it on me – even without knowing what really happened. I mean, had she known and *then* did that, I could understand. But she didn't know–"

"Jamie, either way it goes – whether she knew or not – it was not your fault. But I'm so sorry she treats you that way," I made it a point to remind her.

"They can never be wrong for anything. They never get the blame for a damn thing," Jamie ignored my stance and continued venting. "I mean, it was my fault, but it wasn't *my fault*."

"I will always tell you that it wasn't your fault, Jamie. You couldn't do anything to help that, and you can't do anything to change the decisions they make. The world is not on your shoulders, I promise you," I stared at her, although her eyes were shielded behind troubled eyelids. "Your mom is wrong for acting like it is."

"Thanks, but it just feels that way... A lot," Jamie sighed and finally abandoned that string to look back at me.

"Come to me and I'll help you take the load off," I encouraged her and brushed my fingertips over her hand. I grasped her hand and pulled her forward. She accepted my endeavor and settled her arms around me. Her head rested on my shoulder.

"You're the greatest," Jamie commended me, then leaned back out of my hold. "But anyway, let's get back on track. You want to know me, but I want to know you, too. I feel like you have an unfair advantage because you keep getting me to rant to you. Now it's your turn. Is there anything you feel like you need to get off of your chest?"

"Let me think," I mused as I tried to recall anything bothersome. "Well, I'm kind of bummed out that I have to leave soon. My mom says I can't stay here for the school year, even though I keep begging her to let me."

"You're moving?" Jamie's eyebrows furrowed.

"Well, my parents are divorced. My dad lives here in Savannah, but my mom lives all the way in Atlanta. I don't really like the school I go to up there, and I'd really like to try going to school down here... But my mom says I can't," I provided her with the synopsis of our situation.

"Your parents are divorced?" Jamie tried to keep up. I then realized that perhaps I was guilty of reserving myself just as well.

"Yeah, and I'm staying with my dad right now. I stay with him during the summer and other breaks, but I'm with my mom during the school year," I elaborated a little more. It then occurred to me that she was right, I was never really the one doing the talking, these days. And anything I said revealed nothing about myself, but was instead a response to Jamie.

"I had no idea," Jamie marveled at the fact.

"Really? I figured I've mentioned that before," I paused.

"Nope, it's the first time I've heard that," Jamie countered. "Okay, maybe we should skip the deep stuff for now and focus on learning the basics," Jamie giggled and revised her previous disposition.

I didn't care what we discussed. Jamie was a book, and I was merely flipping through the pages, skipping from chapter to chapter. The thrill was in filling in the blank spaces, connecting the dots. "Okay," I nodded as I giggled as well.

"Where are you from?" Jamie questioned. "I haven't been to your house yet, but you must live close if you work down there at Small Wonder, yeah?"

"Well, I was born in Atlanta. I lived there until I was eleven, when my parents split. But if you mean from around here, I live about fifteen minutes from Small Wonder. My dad drops me off, every day," I answered her in both aspects.

"That makes sense. So then, if you don't mind me asking, are you good with *your* parents? We've never really talked about either set," Jamie introduced her own interrogation.

"Who just sits around and talks about their parents?" I teased her with a downcast smile. "And I mean, the divorce was kind of hard on me, but I've had years to adapt to it and all. It doesn't bother me as much anymore. And I still have a healthy relationship with both of my parents, so it's fine. I love them both, so much. Although I *do* kind of prefer being with my dad, here in Savannah. I love it here."

"How did they end up so far apart? Was it work?" Jamie questioned, so enthused.

"No, actually. My dad used to take me on vacations to Savannah when I was younger to go to Tybee and stuff. We loved going to River Street and seeing all of the historical places and whatnot. And I guess I wasn't the only one that fell in love with it. When my dad moved out, he lived in an apartment for a couple of months, and then he moved out here," I clarified.

"I've been here all my life, so I don't know anything else. I told you that I went to Atlanta for the first time for my Sara concert, but that was it. That's really cool," Jamie nodded receptively.

"It's funny, because everyone thought he had a secret woman on the side or something, but he really just came here because the area brought him peace. It calms me in the same way," I ventured into my past slightly, and Jamie was hanging onto every word that I said. She was so interested, I almost didn't mind having the spotlight on me. "I really wish I could stay."

"That is so sweet. That makes me happy, that everyone is coping well with their situation," Jamie beamed. "But why won't your mom let you stay?"

"She doesn't think my dad is responsible enough to handle me during school. And I mean, she's *kind of* right... But I can handle myself, you know? I have tons of self discipline and motivation. I know I can do well on my own. Especially knowing that it would be my senior year... I know I would focus on what I need to."

"Maybe she's worried about the pressure of going to a new school – on top of your dad. I mean, you seem like you'd be fine with making new friends and all," Jamie marveled at the ability she felt like she lacked, herself.

"Yeah, that's never been a problem for me. I love being around new people. And I don't really like the kids I go to school with now. They're close–minded individuals... Really ignorant about everything that I care about. They don't understand the premise of The Black Lives Matter movement or LGBT legislation or women's rights or... Anything that matters. And I have friends there and everything, but we're so outnumbered, its ridiculous. People are different, down here," I explained briefly, although I could've ranted to Jamie about several injustices and arguments I'd been in.

"That must be awful. That sucks, I'm sorry babe. But I'm pretty sure you can hold your own for one more year. And then you can move back out here and go to college and stuff."

"Yeah... I don't hate it, but I'm really tired of the same thing. But I guess it doesn't matter. I'll have to go back. And you're right, it's just for another year."

"Well, now I guess we'll just have to make every day count," Jamie took the news in stride and caressed my chin.

"We're doing a great job of that, so far," I grinned and leaned into her hand. "I'm so glad I met you."

"Right? I'm glad I decided to start going back to Small Wonder."

"Oh, yeah. Speaking of Small Wonder..." I introduced another pressing question I'd had for some time now. "Okay, Jamie. I have to ask. I've been wondering this since way before I even became interested in you..."

"I don't know why I just got nervous, but go ahead... Ask me," Jamie said uncertainly.

"Where the hell do you work?" I blurted out. "Because, those albums are actually kind of expensive and I work there and I *still* don't buy albums because they cost so much. Yet you can afford to buy one every single day? Doesn't add up. So, which bank are you robbing?"

Jamie laughed a simplistic laugh and placed her hand on my thigh. "I work... It's summer. I work and I don't go anywhere or do anything, so I don't have anything else to spend it on..."

"Define work," I narrowed my eyes at her. "Are you a hitman? Part of the Mafia? Drug dealer?"

"I'm a junior editor," she answered blithely.

"A junior editor?" I repeated curiously.

"It's a summer position I landed right before I graduated. I was searching all throughout senior year for an internship I would like, and I found this. What I do is – Well, I'm kind of like a glorified proofreader. Companies send stuff to go through me before they post things on their websites, or send their emails, or publish their advertisements. It's pretty cool and I get paid well. It's not exactly what I want to be doing – I'd rather be reading manuscripts and editing *those*... But hey, you have to start somewhere," Jamie shared with me animatedly and seemed so enthused with her job. I watched her with bright eyes as she further articulated her words with her hands.

"That's so cool, Jamie! I'm so happy for you. That sounds perfect," I grinned.

"Yeah, it really is..." Jamie agreed. "I used to work in retail, but I got fired for lack of enthusiasm or something... They fired me because of depression, really. Even though they knew what I was going through..." Jamie shrugged. "But, whatever. I really love what I get to do now. I can work from home and I don't have to interact with many people. It's like an internship, and if I do well, I can start from here and build myself up to a higher, more permanent position. We haven't talked about it, but I want to do something in publishing. I love to read, and I think this would be the best job for me. It'll be most ideal, at least. So, that's where I'm working now."

"I'm so jealous, wow. It sounds like a dream," I sighed contentedly for her.

"It really is, and it pays so well. It's beautiful," Jamie beamed. "I get paid weekly with direct deposit. With just an hour of my time, I can buy an album. It's really nothing at all."

"I guess that answers my question..." I trailed, although no job truly paid that well. Not well enough to buy a daily album. "I've done the math, though, Jamie, and that's a lot of money you spend on a weekly basis..."

"We got a *lot* of money for the settlement, initially. He killed my brother, of course we got paid. And when we did, and the funeral was paid for, along with all of the other stuff we had to take care of – I asked for some to pay my dues in my own way. My family knows what I do for him. They don't say anything about it. I asked for money to buy him a CD and they let me. I wanted to do it again, and again, and again, because it just made me feel better, A-L. They gave me enough to let me do it for a while. And I recently bought Corey an entire CD stand to organize all of them for him. I put it in his room," she elaborated and I dwelled on how selfless it was of her. When I registered that it was only due to her guilt, it saddened me. She wouldn't have seen it the way I did.

"Oh, that makes sense. That's really nice of you," I praised her decision and kept my assessment to myself.

"Yeah... It's just something I have to do," Jamie nodded, seeming more subdued and reflective now. "But then, I thought that maybe I shouldn't be using what's technically *his* money to buy him the albums... So, I stopped asking and I just use my own money. I've always been working and I've always had my own money, so I just kept continuing what I was doing. I manage my money. Buying the albums are important to me, so I set aside my own money for it now. When I can afford it, and I usually can, I do it. It makes me feel like shit to go without doing it."

Although I disagreed with her motives, I really did think what she was doing was beautiful. "That's really sweet, babe. I think he would be really happy, if he was still here."

"Yeah," she agreed quietly. "I think about that a lot – If he was still here."

"When did– Um, when did it happen? If you don't mind me asking..." I tried to get a firmer grasp on her situation. I only had bits and pieces of the story.

"It'll be a year on July nineteenth," Jamie said solemnly with a bowed head. I gauged the current date and registered that it was a couple of weeks from now.

The time frame matched my memory. I'd always seen her with the boy I could now identify as Corey, before. It wasn't a daily occurrence like it was now, but they came often. They were undoubtedly our best customers. She'd stopped coming towards the middle of July of last year. At the time, I didn't think anything of it. Perhaps they'd gotten their fix of our store together. Perhaps they'd moved. There were several plausible explanations for their absence, but their involvement in the accident never occurred to me. I suppose I can finally fill in the blanks now.

I didn't have much time to stick around after the accident. I moved back in with my mom around that time and continued with my life. I hadn't seen the accident happen, it happened on one of my days off. But I'd heard about it. I'd heard his name in the talk of the town and in the news, but I'd forgotten because he was a stranger to me. I'd never *seen* who the victim was, and the recurring name: Corey Holden didn't strike me. I wouldn't say it was indifference, because I did care and I was concerned, but it wasn't life–altering news for me. I was shaken for a few days at best, then I moved on. It hurt my heart that Jamie couldn't say the same.

"I'll be there for you, if you want me to be," I offered meagerly, uncertain of another way to respond.

"I'll probably need you," Jamie said and her mood had receded into that solemn poise she usually had about herself.

"Well, I'm always here," I promised and Jamie finally made eye contact with me. I hadn't seen her eyes in a few minutes now.

Jamie stared at me and I guess she was trying to assess the weight of my words. I didn't know of any friends she had, I could gauge the hostility and tension within her family, and she didn't seem to participate in anything outside of work, so I assumed she didn't have much of a network. I wouldn't leave her to muddle through her distress on her own any longer. Jamie would not suffer in silence or torture herself about this when that day arrived. I wouldn't let her. I was determined to be her shoulder to cry on. All she needed was support, and that was the least I could offer to her.

"Thank you," Jamie said clearly after a moment. "I'm glad you are. It'll take me a little while to get used to this, but... Thank you."

"You don't have to thank me, Jamie," I shook my head. "But what do you mean? It'll take you a little while to get used to what?"

"Someone being here for me, every day," Jamie disclosed and she seemed embarrassed by the fact. "I mean, of course I've had friends and stuff... And they were helping me through it as best as they could, but after a certain amount of time... There's nothing they can do. You can only hug someone so much, you know?"

"I've always wondered where your friends were. I mean – You're fantastic. I knew you'd had friends, before... But they just drifted apart?" I tried to follow.

"No... I don't know, not really. Depression hit hard and they didn't know how to deal with it. They'd wanna help and be around, but I wouldn't want them to be. I would just bring down the room wherever I went, and I didn't want to do that anymore, so I just cut off contact. It was never their fault. It wasn't like they just left me – I pushed them away. And they resisted, but gave in eventually. I hate that I did that. They were really great friends... But now it's like – I don't know how to get that back."

"Don't you have their numbers?" I frowned. "You don't have to be around them to keep a friendship. You don't text or call anyone?"

"Yeah, but you know how it is. You run out of conversation really fast when you're living two separate lives. My one friend, Sophie, would always wanna tell me about things going on at her school, and it was like – I wouldn't have any reference. The every day, insignificant stories you tell aren't interesting if they don't know and don't experience it with you. Not that it's not *interesting* – but it's like – You can't tell a funny story to someone that wasn't there. You end up discrediting it with "you had to be there" and it's awkward, you know? And then *I* wouldn't have any stories in return or anything to talk about at all because I haven't even gone to college yet. So... We all kinda drifted like that," Jamie articulated to me in a reminiscent daze.

"Yeah, I know what you mean. I've lost a couple of friends that way," I related. "That's the worst way to lose someone. I always wish we could've had a fight or they did something to me so I could justify losing the friendship. It hurts when you both just grow apart."

"It's not the worst way," Jamie retorted under her breath. "But, yeah."

"But it's summer, now. Surely all of your old friends aren't taking summer classes. How many are still around?" I questioned mischievously. I had a plan.

"I've seen them all around," Jamie mumbled unenthusiastically. "We waved."

"The next time you see them, you should say hi. You can rekindle those friendships. All doesn't have to be lost," I said optimistically. I'd love to expand Jamie's network. I'd love to meet the people she'd been close with, before everything. We could all be friends.

"They all went to college and have pretty much moved on. It's been a *long* time, A-L. Coming back now would be just like meeting a brand–new person. We've missed so much with each other that it's just like... Kind of pointless, I guess. Losing my friends made not speaking to anyone super easy, too," Jamie reverted to her usual mindset. "That's why I'm glad *you* haven't gotten tired of me, yet. I've gotta keep you around. Thank you for putting up with me. It hasn't been that long, but, you know. Thanks."

"Putting up with you," I mocked her and waved her off. This wasn't charity work. "I love being around you. You are my favorite person. Spending time with you is just me indulging on my favorite person. You don't have to thank me."

"It's everything to me," she told me for the second time, and once again, I couldn't help but believe her. Such a simplistic phrase was loaded with sentiment. Jamie scooted closer to me on the bed and wrapped both arms around me. I succumbed to her warmth immediately and hugged her back tightly. The connotation went unsaid, but I understood it through the silence.

"Um–" Jamie said to fill the air. "Are you hungry?"

"Not really, I ate a little while ago."

"Well, what's your favorite food, A-L?" Jamie questioned to get back into the groove we had before we'd deviated. She wanted to change the subject, and I let her.

"That's one of those questions you said we couldn't ask," I playfully admonished her. "For more reasons than one."

"What's the other reason?" she asked playfully.

"I can't choose just one, and if I do, it always changes."

"Oh, yeah," Jamie related. "I'm like that with music. I never have an overall favorite song. I always have to give you like two or three and it'll be different in a week."

"What's on the playlist for this week, then?" I broached and brought my legs up on the bed to cross. Jamie repositioned herself too and grabbed her phone to show me.

Following that new revelation, our conversations never ceased. Jamie was one of those brilliant people that could engage you for hours. Topics flowed seamlessly from one to the next. We shared stories and delved into our lives more than I would've initially given her credit for. And we actually *talked*. It seemed like I'd finally found someone that could perfectly match my intellect level, without arrogance. I was guilty of dumbing myself down and accommodating a lot for the people that surrounded me, but Jamie gave me the strangest urge to be myself.

The connection we shared was much deeper than that of just friends, or even girlfriends. I felt like Jamie could understand me as a person. She was there with me. My mindset was scarily close to hers. She got me in a way no one else could. I'd never experienced love the way it had always been described. I'd never been so pleased with the overall essence of a person so deeply. No individual had ever commanded my attention like Jamie did, and I'd never given it so willingly. Jamie was teaching me how naturally it all could occur. Falling for someone happened steadily. No fanfare was needed. The sensations spoke for themselves. It wouldn't have to be questioned, nor announced.

Feelings of love undoubtedly started to blossom that night, but suddenly I wasn't scared of that possibility anymore. It would be a pleasure to fall in love with Jamie Holden.

Anna

My dad started to catch on, eventually. Jamie and I had been kind of inseparable. She wasn't one that I wanted to keep away from my father, but it came across that way when I spent more and more time away from the house. He knew of Jamie. I was constantly talking about her. He joked that he was starting to think that she was a figment of my imagination, that I'd made her up. It then dawned on me that I hadn't made it a point to bring her around. And I should've.

"Babe, do you have any plans later on today?" I asked Jamie when she stopped by, keeping up her daily routine. In fact, she'd been arriving much earlier. Hours earlier.

"Do I ever have plans?" she playfully flipped the question back on me, leaning closer to me over the counter.

"Well, I have somewhere I want us to go," I made a cheeky suggestion and Jamie tapped me on the nose.

"Is it another date?" she inferred and couldn't shake that grin. Everything about her was so bright.

"Not really, this time. No," I shook my head. "You haven't met my dad yet. You haven't been to my house. Everything we do happens either at your house or out somewhere. I haven't brought you home, yet."

"I know," Jamie acknowledged. I sensed the but.

"But you haven't mentioned it, because?" I prompted her.

"I thought maybe you were avoiding it for some reason. I wasn't going to corner you by asking or anything, I just figured that if you wanted me over, you'd ask me to come," Jamie shrugged. "Because you never invited me – and I wasn't gonna invite myself."

"You're always making these plans and coordinating all of these little dates after work. It just never crossed my mind. There was no real reason behind it," I laughed freely at her perception along with her sensitivity for the subject. "Are you free to come over today? When I'm off?"

"Let's go right now," Jamie suggested cheekily and reached for my hands.

"I don't think that's a good idea. Cassie's been really nice about you, and us, and letting us go out and everything, but I don't want to take advantage of that – You know? I literally haven't stayed for my whole shift all week. We keep doing things and she keeps letting us, but I feel like I should hold up my end of this job, too."

"Oh, no I understand, A-L. You keep working and we can go later. Do you want me to drop by later?" Jamie proactively adapted to my suggestion.

"I'm not saying I want you to leave, I just don't think we should keep leaving in the middle of my shift. You can stay, love, it's okay," I settled my hand over her forearm.

"Okay," she smiled her relief.

"And I mean, it's not like Cassie has to pull my weight a whole lot without me here... But still. You know it doesn't get very busy, but I just feel guilty about always leaving her here... Even though she gives me permission, I just feel like I shouldn't. I don't know," I digressed and looked back to the woman that was entertaining herself with her headphones in, scrolling through her phone. She was hunched over the crate of albums she should've been sorting through. This wasn't a particularly demanding job either way.

"I totally get you. We *have* been kind of taking advantage of it, but I can't help it. I love going out with you. I look forward to our adventures every day," Jamie shared candidly.

"Me too, oh my God. And that's why my dad thinks you're probably not even real," I shook my head in amusement. "We're always on adventures."

"He thinks I'm not real?" Jamie giggled.

"He's never seen you. He's only heard about you," I laughed at his logic. "After I leave your house, I come back here for him to pick me up. And I'll tell him that I was at your house and he'll give me this look, like, *yeah right*."

"I'm an urban legend," Jamie shrugged.

"A myth," I continued.

"I'm all in your head, A-L. I hate to break it to you," Jamie teased and brushed her knuckle over my chin.

"Bummer. I kind of knew this was too good to be true," I played along.

"Things can be good, and true," Jamie promised me cryptically, then pitched forward to steal a kiss. She'd grasped me just under my jaw and her hands framed my face. After staring at me in wonder, she dropped her hands.

"Yes, yes they can be," I seconded in that post–kiss stupor I kept falling into. Jamie kept luring me into that same trance, but it didn't feel as if I were being lured at all. It was a pull I succumbed to, willingly. Always willingly.

This was a lovely cycle we were developing. I liked to separate myself from the moment to assess where we were. Together, we were actively cultivating this. We were both working towards an "*us*" just as diligently as the other.

Nothing was forced. We could avoid those tense, compulsive conversations about reciprocation – having to wonder, day to day, the juvenile question of whether she still likes me; whether I was the only one; whether those feelings were authentic or temporary. They were unnecessary when we both so clearly expressed our feelings – without words.

Through the mutual light in our eyes and the brightening of our features after every hug, there is validation. Escaping in every shy giggle after staring too long is the certainty that, yes, this is happening – that she's feeling it, too. Between every airtight clasp of our hands and tentative embrace of our bodies, that tenacity, that gentle pause, that delicate moment of – is this okay? is she alright with this? – says far more than we could, verbally. Our pacing is one in the same. And there are no rules, but if there were, we are doing this the right way. As it should be.

Jamie stuck around until the end of my shift. I had the feeling she would. We entertained each other for two and a half hours, with nothing but each other. Conversation was our only tool, and we utilized it. We debated. We debated about whether lemonade was classified as a juice or its own entity, whether the correct term is 'politics is' or 'politics are', and even whether toothpaste's intent is to freshen breath or for tooth health. We came to an agreement that both applied. We shared stories and divulged more insignificant details about our lives. Jamie told me more about that Sara Bareilles concert I'd missed out on and we bonded over other artists. Our discussions were never interrupted as we milled about the store. When we approached the instruments, I discovered that Jamie played a little bit of piano, as I did with guitar. She played a little bit of *Piano Man* and in turn, I played some of *Here Comes the Sun*. We talked. We laughed. We enjoyed each other. Everything flowed so seamlessly. It always did.

Our fun paused when Cassie sauntered over to tell me that it was okay to clock out. After doing so, Jamie and I made our way outside to sit on our bench. "I guess I should call my dad and tell him he can come pick us up," I announced and pulled out my phone. "You got permission to come over, right?"

"Yeah," Jamie shrugged indefinitely, but something told me that she hadn't asked at all. I knew that she assumed her family wasn't too concerned, but I wanted them to know where she was regardless. I knew they cared for her.

"Well, okay," I digressed and called my dad. We talked briefly, just enough to get the message across.

"You didn't say anything about *we*," Jamie emphasized.

"I want him to see you for himself," I smirked to myself. "He'll be here soon."

"So, it's a surprise?" she laughed softly.

"Precisely," I nodded and leaned into her. Jamie placed her arm around me and leaned her head against mine. We were in a comfortable silence on an uncomfortable bench.

"What do you think he'll say?" Jamie shifted to look at me.

"What is there to say?" I returned.

"I don't know. I'm just kind of nervous. *I'm meeting your dad*," Jamie emphasized as if it were some big occasion.

Perhaps I hadn't felt that stress because I hadn't intended to meet her parents, not really. I was going for Jamie, not to impress her family. I hadn't thought of it as *meeting the parents*. I hadn't thought of them at all, until Margaret walked in. And even then, I didn't feel myself posing a problem nor Margaret posing a threat. It was a natural occurrence to me, as it should've been for Jamie.

"Don't be, he's cool," I admonished her and held onto her arm. I thought that should've been the end of it. Things were never that simple.

"I am, though. What if he doesn't like me?" Jamie insisted on brooding about it.

"He'll like you, babe," I insisted and caught her worried eye.

"What if he–" Jamie broached, then stopped herself. That jovial light in her eyes had gone. I'd watched it dissipate.

"What?" I wondered with a knitted brow.

"What if he asks me about the accident?" she said in an almost haunted whisper.

"He wouldn't. Even if he knows who you are, he won't say anything. He's not like that. You don't have anything to worry about, Jamie, I promise," I appeased her and placed my hand on her knee. But Jamie was in her state again. I was going to have a trying time at getting her out of it.

"You know you're the only one I talk to. I don't talk in public because when people recognize me, they want to stare and sometimes they want to ask questions. They think they're entitled to answers after being nosey. That's all that ever happened when it was still fresh..." Jamie voiced her distant fears and wouldn't look at me, nor acknowledge my touch.

"My dad won't ask you any questions about that. He'll ask you the usual, dumb parent things like 'how's school?' and stuff. He'll ask about how we met... He'll ask about *you*, Jamie, not Corey's accident..." I tried to assure her, but she wasn't hearing me.

"He's from around here, you're not. You wouldn't really have a grasp on a small–town dynamic, being from Atlanta. Everyone around here knows what happened. They know who we are, most likely. I just don't want to be reminded of it, tonight. I feel like I can get away from it with you, and even Cassie... But I just thought of having to talk to him, too. Having him talk to me... I don't know what he's going to say. That just scared me again," Jamie shared with me honestly as she trapped her hands between her thighs and sunk into herself.

"News isn't news forever, Jamie. Don't take this the wrong way, but, it's not that recent. You guys aren't celebrities. I'm pretty sure there's no paparazzi standing around, waiting to get a statement from you. No one's shoving a microphone in your face. You shouldn't have to feel threatened or cornered by the possibility of someone talking to you. You're more than the accident. Your family is more than the accident. It doesn't define you," I tried to emphasize, to no avail. I didn't want to tell her outright that she was being irrational, but she was.

"I don't know, A-L. It just feels that way," she pursed her lips and dropped the subject.

Jamie was damaged. My feelings for her couldn't make that fact any less true. Although it wasn't all I saw when I looked at her, it was there. It couldn't be ignored – especially when she had her moments. The accident and Corey in general had left such a void within her, and a gaping hole in her family. With Jamie, there was no differentiation. She couldn't seem to separate herself from the tragedy. That guilt was embedded in her. It had consumed her. She couldn't put it behind her. She couldn't move on. Having the privilege of distracting her only amounted to a brief bout of relief from her demons. This unwarranted reaction only served to emphasize that she was dealing with this on a much larger scale than I'd initially assumed. It frightened me, because there was no talking her out of it.

I only hugged her. I didn't give her a choice as I settled my arms around her. She stiffened for a moment. Thankfully, Jamie received me. I wanted to heal her. I wanted to relieve her of her suffering – that perpetual suffering. Even if only for a little while. As Jamie allowed me to hug her and she finally hugged me back, I rubbed along the length of her spine. She curled into me and set her chin on my shoulder. I took it as her thanks.

Headlights then illuminated the two of us as my dad pulled up. I held onto Jamie for a second longer, because I was not ashamed of her. I hugged her until I felt that our hug was complete. It was not impeded by his presence, nor the lights on us. I wanted Jamie to know that the way I cared for her was not only behind her closed bedroom door, or within the quiet music shop, or in a secluded area of a park. It knew no boundaries and neither did I. Jamie was made bashful from our audience of one. My dad made her withdraw from me, but I didn't mind much. I'd conveyed my own message.

"There he is. Are you ready?" I dropped my arms and gestured to him.

"I guess," Jamie mumbled. There was more protesting in her expression, but she didn't bother verbalizing it.

"Try to relax," I squeezed her thigh before getting up.

"Hey," I greeted my dad after hoisting myself up in his grey Chevy pickup truck. "I brought a friend with me."

He quirked his eyebrow when he looked past me, although he didn't show any outward signs of surprise. But I'd seen it. I wondered what had surprised him. He knew Jamie's gender, her age. What could've shocked him? As I considered myself and the gorgeous girl behind me, it occurred to me.

Though I had skin much fairer than she, I found similarities between the two of us. My hair was straighter and a shade or two lighter, but fell around my shoulders just the same. My eyes were a lighter brown, hazel - if you will, but they saw the same things. Her lips were fuller than mine, but we spoke the same language. My nose was narrower, straighter than hers, yet we still inhaled each other. Jamie and I were different, sure. But we were one in the same. The difference in the color of our skin didn't change that.

It was a split-second inference, but I'd noticed. He'd probably assumed she was also white. But just as soon as it registered that she was not, he'd accepted her without hesitance. I appreciated that.

"Would that be this mysterious Jamie I keep hearing about?" he smirked and leaned over to see her better as she bashfully stayed on the sidewalk.

"It is," I happily supplied. "Told you she was real."

"Well, I see that now. Nice to meet you, Jamie. Hop on in," he greeted her warmly and nudged me. "Scoot over."

I gladly made room and met Jamie's uncertain gaze. Silently, she heaved herself up and into the seat next to me. We were sitting snugly. Our hips were touching, hers wider than mine. I was conscious of how close she was to me. She didn't look at me.

"Buckle up," he instructed us and slowly drove off. We passed the rest of the storefront and came to a red light. "So, I'm guessing tonight's a pizza night."

"Yes!" I cheered discreetly, keeping in mind our proximity. Having someone over was synonymous with pizza.

"How's pizza sound, Jamie?" he asked her directly, and I held my breath. I hoped she would reply. She hadn't said anything thus far.

In the red glow of the stop light, our faces were only slightly illuminated. The streetlights didn't reach into his pickup and there wasn't enough light to detect features, but when Jamie nodded, he could see it. He smiled and focused his gaze ahead, back on the road. It wasn't meant to be confrontational in the slightest when I turned to look at Jamie. It wasn't confrontational anyway, because Jamie wasn't allowing herself to be confronted. She'd retreated into that same sullen posture with her hands between her thighs. She was looking out of the window. I pursed my lips, already knowing exactly how this night would go.

It only took my dad two more attempts at starting a conversation and having Jamie respond wordlessly to give up on it. He'd asked her what she wanted on her pizza, to which she shrugged. And I'd had to supply him with a verbal answer about how she didn't mind any toppings. Between the two of them, I tried to keep everything as natural as possible. I answered for her, when I had to. I kept conversation up with my dad because I knew how. I was giving Jamie a pass. He asked me about work and if anyone new had come in today. I answered a few, but that we could always count on Jamie. He smiled at her as we neared our house, turning into our neighborhood.

Jamie returned his smile, and I knew the difference. That was the same polite smile she'd always given me day to day – that guarded smile, that apologetic smile as if to say *this is all you're getting out of me tonight, sorry*. After having elicited her gorgeous, authentic smiles on so many occasions, seeing this one unsettled me. I wanted her to make progress. She seemed to have relapsed.

In the final minute or two of our ride, I simply hoped for the best. Jamie wasn't speaking again, my dad had learned not to try, and I was worrying about why she was worrying. I'd messed up in springing that on her. I should've talked it through with her. But I had – hadn't I? Those signs – that fear – was not present when I broached the subject. None of it was. She seemed happy, and like she'd been looking forward to it. She'd made me feel as though this was something that was delayed, something that should've been out of the way ages ago. Why would she go about it so differently when it was happening? When she had the chance to make that first impression, she'd frozen. And I didn't know why.

Jamie was determined to keep her gaze out of the window. I figured that she was disassociating. She wasn't in the truck with us. No, she was elsewhere. Somewhere where my dad was not – where there was no stranger. Where there was no threat. Where there was no uncertainty. I hoped that wherever she was, I was there with her as well. Somehow.

The bumping of us pulling into our driveway jolted Jamie out of whatever trance she'd induced herself in. She slowly turned around to face me – and it was so unwilling. I loathed that I'd noticed such a thing. She pursed her lips and waited for him to turn off the engine before she meagerly got out. We didn't say anything. Neither of knew how to fill the silence she'd forced on us yet again.

"I'll go ahead and call in the pizza. You sure anything's alright? This one likes *pineapples* on hers," he warned Jamie while making a face at my very delicious preference.

"Hush," I admonished him back and looked to Jamie for her final shot at round one. My beanied girl gave him that same subdued quirk of her lips and shrugged her indifference yet again, shifting her gaze to the floor.

"Alright," he took it in stride and wandered off to find the pizza parlor's number on the refrigerator.

"We can go upstairs," I gestured towards the staircase and Jamie fell into step with me.

I led the way and checked on her every few steps, although I heard her modest footsteps right behind mine. I had an overwhelming desire to make sure she was alright. I usually never had that urge, although she was still the same Jamie as always. Slipping back into her silence ignited that protective compulsion. I'd just looked over my shoulder again as I followed along that same path that was so familiar to me, but all new to Jamie. I paused just outside of my door, resting my hand on the doorknob. I took a breath and pushed the door open, inviting her in.

My room was pretty mundane. It looked just about like any other girl's room my age. I'd always wished it had more personality. I never really had that stroke of creativity enough to give it any. And I was only here during the summers, so it was kind of okay for it to be so plain. I didn't want to put so much effort into it, only to leave it by the time I'd be satisfied with it. Jamie's expression was willing to discredit everything I'd thought about my room. There was such a pleasant look on her face, such content wonder. She looked like she was exploring something completely magical as she allowed herself further in my room. I watched her taking it all in. She was beautiful.

That real smile had made its return. I liked to call it *my* smile. I was usually the one that put it there, and it was much different from the one she'd given my dad. Jamie looked up at my few posters – I'd always had to bring one home from a concert. Then she looked at my poor excuse of a shrine for my friends, both from Atlanta and the few I'd made here. I briefly imagined a wall filled with Jamie and things we'd yet to do, documenting the adventures we'd yet to go on. I was imagining our spot on my blank wall, right above my bed. Or perhaps on the wall with the door. Maybe on my closet. I was avidly making plans for it when Jamie broke the quiet in her peculiar way.

"I don't mind pineapples," Jamie shared with me once she was closed in my room. "I actually kind of like them. It's a nice contrast."

"Yeah, it's a little sweetness in there with the rest. It's my favorite," I nodded, almost startled by her sudden speaking.

"The perfect balance," Jamie nodded to herself and took a seat on my bed. I could see her deflecting from the conversation I wasn't going to make her have.

"Yeah. What's your favorite kind of pizza? The one you prefer?" I continued on with this topic, because it was what she wanted. She'd rather talk about pizza than her lapse in the car. I didn't mind letting her.

"I mean, you can never go wrong with cheese or pepperoni," she answered distractedly. I followed her gaze and it led me to a photograph of my mom and I. "You look just like her."

"People always say that. I think I look more like my dad," I shrugged and sat down next to her.

"I think I look like my dad, too," Jamie pressed on.

"I can see both," I concluded after I studied her, visualizing her both of her parents. "Your mom, a little more."

"That's probably because you've seen my mom more often," Jamie laughed under her breath at nothing. She was clearly running out of excess conversation to make. We both felt that confrontation creeping nearer. But she was determined to prolong it, still.

"No, I've seen your dad a couple of times enough to have a solid schema," I disagreed. "I still think you look like him more."

"Nice psychology reference."

"I'm glad you knew what I was talking about."

"Psychology was my favorite class, senior year," Jamie persisted in talking about other things. I would let her dance around the issue until her feet ached.

"I took it my junior year. I actually just took the AP exam. I guess you could say things are still pretty fresh."

"I took the AP exam, too."

"What'd you make?"

"A four."

"I think I probably made a three. I did better in AP lit."

"I never took that one."

"It was pretty easy."

"Yeah..." Jamie trailed off and looked to me, as if she was expecting that dreaded segue. I wasn't going to give it to her. I didn't want her first night at my house to go awry. I wanted this to be a good memory of ours. We could save the tears and the heavy talks for the bench, some other night. Those emotions had no place here.

I held her gaze, but it was not awkward. We were both looking, silently assessing. I'd had ample time to master the practice, but there was always something more to notice. That beanie was barely clinging onto her head. It had been sliding off, the way she wore it halfway off of her head. Before it had the chance to escape, I simply reached over and pulled it back snugly. Jamie broke into a smile of both confusion and gratitude. It lingered as I fixed her hair back for her, the wispy way she always wore it.

"Thanks," she breathed when I finished.

"You're welcome," I beamed. "I love it, by the way."

"My beanie?"

"Yeah."

"It's Corey's, actually," Jamie admitted. "But I like to wear it. Always have him with me, you know."

"It looks great on you," I nodded my approval once again and drank her in.

"Thanks," she repeated meekly and looked down at her lap.

I continued to look at her, noticing the mundane details. Her mundane details – like the slight bump in the curve of her nose and the tiniest mole just beneath it. That small pimple just above her eyebrow. The few hairs that had grown back around her usually plucked eyebrows. I noted how dangerous it was that I was romanticizing her blemishes and imperfections, but Jamie had overwhelming artistry even when it shouldn't have been viewed as such. Despite the fact that I saw her father and she saw her mother, they'd both collaborated to make one hell of a girl. My girl.

"Why aren't you asking me?" Jamie gave up and addressed it herself. I was surprised. I thought we were looking at each other when in fact, I was admiring her and she was merely waiting on me.

"It's not my thing to ask. You'd tell me if you wanted to," I gave an earnest response. "But you don't owe me any explanations."

"I mean, I made it awkward in the car so in a way, I kind of do. I was just waiting for you to ask me why I didn't talk," Jamie said guiltily. "This whole time I've been trying to figure out what the hell I was gonna say."

"You don't owe me anything. Jamie, I know how hard change can be, and how scary it can be – for you especially. I wasn't really expecting anything in particular. I went into it knowing that it could go one of two ways. Either you would speak, or you wouldn't. You chose not to. There's nothing to explain. I get it," I shrugged it off. I wasn't upset with her.

"I wanted to... But I just couldn't," Jamie stressed and looked away again. I gauged how disappointed she was in herself.

"It's okay, babe. I'll tell my dad what's going on and it'll allow you to figure him out on your own time. You can wait to talk to him as long as you want to," I suggested.

"No," Jamie declined instantly.

"No, what?" I faltered. "He's really understanding and he wouldn't pressure you–"

"I don't want that. That's... Unnecessary, A-L. I should be able to talk to him like a normal person, and I can. I just freaked out last time and–"

"I know. That's why I said that... I don't want you to be out of your comfort zone, babe," I placed my hand on her knee.

"My comfort zone is ridiculous, though, Anna. This isn't normal. I'm only comfortable with you. That whole elective mutism thing is so annoying – even to me. I'll want to talk, and make new friends, and meet new people... But trying to prepare myself for what they'll say next just terrifies me. I have no way of knowing where a conversation is headed. I don't want to put myself in the position to be asked about Corey, so I just don't. It's anxiety. Instead of talking and letting the conversation get to that point, I'd rather avoid it altogether. And I want to overpower it, but sometimes it's just too hard," Jamie struggled to articulate, and I wanted to help her believe that she didn't need to.

"Ridiculous or – *normal* – or not, I still care about how you feel. I don't want you to go through any unnecessary stress or anxiety... I'm just saying, there's no rush. You don't have to do anything you don't want to do, especially not for me or my dad," I concluded and retracted my hand.

"Well, I want to. Maybe I will one day."

What a familiar phrase. Hearing it verbally put the brightest smile on my face. I tried to suppress it, but I ended up laughing. Leave it to Jamie to make me so bubbly without any intentions of doing so at all.

"What?" a smile crept onto her lips involuntarily from my display.

"I'm just really happy," I excused myself as my giggles faded. Jamie had no idea of the effect she had on me.

"What happened?" she raised a quizzical eyebrow.

"Don't you remember?" I paused, and her blank look gave me my answer. "You wrote that to me, back when I had to talk to you through that little notepad. It's just kind of funny to *hear* you say that, now."

"I remember, now," Jamie nodded with a reminiscent grin.

"I remember when I thought I was never going to hear your voice," I peeked up and shared a vulnerable moment with her. Our atmosphere had shifted, now. As I stared into my favorite brown eyes, and I finally saw that same adoration I was getting used to, I knew the moment had passed. "I'm glad you let me in."

"I'm glad you were persistent," Jamie pitched forward and kissed me between my eyebrows. Then, she sat closer to me. She was inviting me back into her vicinity.

"And I remember when I thought that we'd never be friends," I laughed at my frantic, overly obsessive past. I would over analyze our every interaction, criticize my every move, speculate what was going through her mind.

"Well, guess what happened," Jamie grinned and took my hand symbolically.

"All I wanted was to be your friend, and I got so much more," I realized as she slipped her fingers between the spaces in mine and tightened her grip. Because I felt so inclined, and because I had the liberty, I leaned over and kissed her cheek.

"And I remember when I thought I'd never get to kiss you," I continued and eyed the area my lips had just touched, how it faintly shimmered with the Chapstick I was wearing. I marveled at my insignificant mark on her, and the fact that Jamie had let me leave it.

"I remember thinking that, too," Jamie admitted with her focus trained directly on my lips. "And I remember how amazing it felt when I finally got to do it."

"It *did* feel pretty amazing," I gushed.

"I want to feel it again," Jamie shared as she began to close the distance between us. She was already in close proximity, just sitting next to me, and she leaned closer still until our lips were touching. They merely brushed, then they moulded.

Tilted at an angle, she ravished my mouth. I was consumed in a frenzy of lips, tongue, and teeth. Thirty seconds in, and I felt the need to catch my breath. When I did, it was of Jamie. Every hasty breath I inhaled was filled with Jamie's essence.

I'd kissed Jamie quite a few times since we'd been acquainted, but I hadn't *kissed* Jamie. She was *kissing* me now.

Jamie's hand had found its place on my side, just above my hip. I liked it there. As she unnerved me with her mouth, she caressed and consoled me with her touch. It skirted along my side, ghosting over my shirt and skin without daring to deviate. I found that her figure was far more entrancing up close, and apparently, she was under the same impression. I was pulled, slightly – tentatively, into her frame. Closer, then further as she laid me down. Chest to chest. We were indulging, then. With her above me and our bodies closer than they had been, we became impassioned. I had to steel myself against the mattress as she angled herself into me. Then I steeled myself beneath her, succumbing to both the press of her mouth and her body. My hand rested on the nape of her neck as we experienced each other in this new way. Her hand persisted along my side, with more deliberation. Perhaps things might've escalated, save the doorbell's interruption.

"Pizza's here!" my dad called up, and just like that, our bubble of euphoria had been severed.

Jamie and I separated breathlessly. What we'd done was our secret. It was mine and hers to keep. Not the ringing of the doorbell, nor my dad, nor the pizza guy, even, could take away what we'd created – that moment.

"Coming!" I acknowledged him, then grabbed Jamie's hand. I tugged her happily along, not concerned with the pending conversation she may or may not have had. It wasn't as important.

Even as we ate, I couldn't keep the images from my mind. Although her advances were not explicitly sexual in nature, there was something erotic about her kiss. She was sensual. Every part of me felt light beneath her delicate touch. I was flying when she kissed me – when she *kissed* me. We shared secret glances across the table with our mouths full. Our mouths had been full of each other, minutes ago.

"So, where'd you pick this one up?" my dad asked Jamie after taking his first few bites. He'd asked his question about how we'd met in his strange, Dad way. I wondered if Jamie would even know what he meant.

Jamie looked at me, then at her pizza. That comfortable, lighthearted Jamie had departed, and timid Jamie was left in her wake. I stopped mid–chew and waited, although I couldn't seem like I was waiting. I tried my best to go unfazed, unaware of whether she was going to respond or not. I couldn't pay too much attention. I was shocked, to say the least, when her quiet voice gave an answer that was barely above a whisper.

"I met her at Small Wonder," she cooperated, and I beamed at her. I also couldn't look like it'd meant too much. But I was so proud of her.

"She's a regular," I seconded.

"Records or CDs?" he questioned again.

"CDs," she answered resolutely. "I got Jackson 5 today."

"My girl," he grinned his approval and Jamie gleamed in light of it. "You kids don't know nothin' about that, though."

"I once did a tap routine to Rockin' Robin. I was in the third grade," she contested respectfully, but challengingly. "So, I'd like to think I know a little bit."

I watched their interaction with a bursting sense of pride. I didn't want my smile to be so obvious, but it was. Jamie didn't seem to mind. She glanced at me and her expression lifted. My dad kept asking her questions and pulling her into a discussion, and Jamie allowed it to happen. She eased her guard tremendously. As they talked – yes, they were *talking* amongst themselves – I stole a lone pen from the table and wrote a friendly note to Jamie on a napkin, then slid it across the table, just out of my dad's view.

I'm proud of you.

Jamie read it discreetly and that light was restored to her eyes. Proud was an understatement. Jamie expertly participated in our conversation. I didn't know if it was the lingering high from our kissing, or some personal revelation, but she'd grown. She spoke to my dad and I and held up her end of the conversation well after we'd consumed our pizza. My dad was scoping her out, and she was doing much of the same. They seemed to like one another. I took it as a personal victory.

"Well, I'll get out of your hair for the night," my dad excused himself and took his paper plate to the garbage. "Jamie, did you plan on staying the night?"

She looked at me for the answer. I looked right back at her. We shared a look that said nothing more than, *if it's alright with you, it's alright with me*. I shrugged and she raised her eyebrows. "Yes."

"See you in the morning, then," he bid us good night and trudged up the stairs.

"Good night," we both echoed him when we were alone at our kitchen table.

Jamie stared at me expectantly, and I returned her gaze full of pride. "You did it."

"I guess I did, didn't I?" she mused and that incredulous grin had returned.

"I knew you could. I believed in you. But if I'm being honest, I didn't think it would be this soon," I admitted. "It's a very pleasant surprise."

"I heard you, what you said up there. And I wanted to, myself. I just wanted to prove it – to both of us," Jamie reasoned and shrugged off her massive achievement.

"Well, I am proud of you. Ridiculously proud," I reiterated and pushed back in my chair. "Want to go back up to my room?"

"Sure," she assented and followed suit.

After cleaning up behind ourselves, we walked the same path back to my room. Jamie closed the door behind her and we were in for the night. Enclosed back in our secret bubble, we were most comfortable with ourselves. Jamie sat on my bed with her legs crossed and I occupied myself on the floor with my back against my closet. We drifted in and out of conversation, every now and then. We weren't always talking, but we didn't have to be. Being here with each other was enough for us.

Sleepover or not, my bed time didn't acclimate. Sleep was calling me half past eleven, and it tickled Jamie that I was tired. "You're like an old woman."

"What can I say? I like my sleep," I mentioned in the midst of gathering my pajamas – or what I classified as pajamas. A tee shirt and fuzzy bottoms sufficed for me. "I can never stay up late, even if I want to. My eyelids just get heavy and I put myself through all of these unnecessary things when I always end up falling asleep anyway."

"I thought we would stay up," Jamie said quietly as I began to strip myself of my shirt. Strangely enough, I wasn't made insecure under her scrutiny as I scrambled to change, standing in front of her in only my bra. I didn't feel anything short of confident as I did so in front her. I wasn't much worth marveling at, but nothing about my body was particularly unattractive. I usually tried to maintain a relatively high image of myself, and her gaze didn't discourage that. She wasn't ogling my figure, but I did have her attention. I didn't mind it.

"For you, I'll try," I compromised once my shirt was over my head. "I can't make any promises that I'll last longer than fifteen minutes."

"You can't go to bed early at a sleepover, A-L," Jamie pushed her case anyway, now that she'd gotten her fix.

"I said I would try," I retorted and dropped my pants, to which Jamie also observed in her quiet manner. This was a part of me she hadn't seen, thus far. I would look on, too.

"We can do something instead of just talking, like wat–"

"If you suggest watching a movie, I might as well tuck myself in and go to sleep right now," I interrupted her metaphorical itinerary in slipping off my jeans.

"Okay, scratch that then," Jamie giggled. "We can... Create something, or play music, go on a walk, or–"

"Jamie, it's eleven o'clock," I deadpanned once the soft fabric was loosely over my hips. "I'm not going on a walk, anywhere."

"So, what? It could be four o'clock in the morning and we could do whatever we wanted to do," Jamie responded with an enigmatic gleam about her. "Since when does time restrain you?"

"When you're thirty seconds late to class and your teacher makes you go get a pass, anyway," I scoffed, still sensitive from my last infractions.

"Okay. Fair point, well made," Jamie paused.

"Thank you," I smirked. "Baby, really – I don't mean to be a party pooper, but I'm really tired. What's so wrong with just laying down and talking?"

"Nothing, I guess. As long as you're up for me to talk to," Jamie digressed reluctantly.

"Fifteen minutes," I reminded her. "That's my goal. Anything less, and you can be mad at me. Anything more, and I have a pass to be grumpy in the morning. Deal?"

"Deal," Jamie grinned despite the compromise and clambered back onto my bed.

"Don't you wanna change?" I questioned when she was in front of me on all fours.

"I didn't bring anything, remember?" she posed and continued to lay herself down.

"You can wear something of mine," I proposed, suddenly shy in my endeavors. I'd always offered pajamas to friends, but this felt more intimate.

"I'd love to," Jamie paused, giving me a winsome smile over her shoulder.

I liked the idea of giving something I owned to Jamie. I liked the idea of her using my things as if they were her own. I liked the idea of sharing; of something being ours.

"I'd love for you to," I seconded and slipped out of bed to fetch her something. Jamie wasn't much bigger than me at all. We could easily fit into each other's clothing. I found a shirt I'd gotten as memorabilia from my anatomy club days and one of my favorite pairs of fuzzy pants. She took them from me graciously.

"Thanks," she beamed and let her gaze linger.

"Of course," I nodded and situated myself on half of my bed. I had a full, here at my dad's house. At my mom's, I was only afforded with a twin bed. Jamie and I could be comfortable tonight and I wouldn't have to feel too overbearing.

"Oh, these are super soft," Jamie mentioned after peeling her pants off and slowly putting mine on. Her hand glided over the material in awe.

"Those are my favorite ones, actually. They're the softest ones I have. They stayed soft even after putting them in the wash," I pulled my knees up to my chest, watching my favorite girl.

"I need to invest in some of these, man," Jamie continued to stroke her hand along her pantleg, and I had images of when she'd done the same motion around my waist.

"Yes, yes you do," I agreed. "This is kind of nice," I announced as I observed her in the same curious way she'd observed me.

"Yeah, it is," Jamie concurred without hesitation and slipped out of her shirt.

"Do you even know what I'm talking about?" I smirked over at her in amusement.

"You're talking about us," Jamie answered intuitively, much to my surprise. My shirt was now surrounding her and I wanted my body to do the same. "And what we've become."

"Yeah," I said pleasantly. "I've never really had this before."

"Really?" Jamie looked surprised and clambered over to me, donned in my clothing.

"Yeah..." I reiterated more consciously.

"You've never dated anyone before?" Jamie turned to me and propped herself up with her elbow. "I mean, seriously. Kindergarten boyfriends and two–week middle school relationships don't count."

"If my sixteen–day relationship with Joey Bradbury in the seventh grade doesn't count, then no," I shared and pursed my lips. That had always been a distant insecurity of mine. My dating history had been relatively stagnant. I didn't actively seek anyone out, so I couldn't really feel too bad about it. That insecurity only resurfaced when people discussed their several boyfriends and girlfriends, like I figured Jamie was preparing to divulge to me.

"I dated this guy for a year and some months. He's really the only one I think counts," Jamie reflected, and suddenly, I didn't feel so bad. She'd only had one. "His name was Travis."

"What happened?" I mused and offered her insight on my own demise. "Joey broke up with me because I wouldn't sit with him and his friends at lunch. I guess that was a real deal–breaker, huh?"

"Sounds like it," she raised her eyebrows. "Travis was moving too fast for me. He was so in love and I just – *wasn't*. He would try to make me love him by doing everything he could and it would just push me away. I don't know. He was sweet, but not for me at the time. I didn't want him, then. I was a sophomore and he was a senior, on top of that. It was just kind of weird for me."

"Do you ever miss him?" I questioned, not out of jealousy, but simple curiosity. "I miss Joey sometimes, but then I think that I don't really have anything to miss. So, there's that."

"Sometimes, but overall... No," Jamie said bluntly.

"Well, okay," I laughed freely and Jamie joined me.

"I mean, I don't really *miss* him... But sometimes, I think about him. He was really good to me. He treated me well. I really broke his heart when I ended it, A-L," Jamie admitted, and I could still sense her guilt from it. "I think about that, and how he's doing now. I hope he's better."

"I know Joey's better," I brought up sardonically, able to laugh at the fact now. "He was just fine, not even a week later. He was kissing someone else like three days after he dumped me."

"Well, Joey is missing out," Jamie scooted closer to me and brushed her thumb over my cheekbone in adoration.

"Definitely," I brought my hand up to mesh with hers, then instinctively intertwined them beneath the sheets.

"I've got a question that you don't necessarily have to answer, but I'm trying to figure out," Jamie broached tentatively.

"You can ask me anything," I granted.

"I'm getting that you like girls and boys... Are you bisexual? Or, I guess I should be asking – if you know – what is your sexuality, exactly?"

"I don't actually know. I've only ever liked one boy, and that was because he liked me first. And then I realized that I didn't even like him because I didn't care when he broke up with me," I tried to explain something I wasn't even sure of, myself. "And I don't get crushes a lot or anything. I mean, I'm attracted to people sometimes, but it's never too deep. I get over things within a week. I don't know, I'm weird. Now that I'm thinking about it, I've really only liked you."

"Sounds like a Jamiesexual," Jamie said with a philosophic glow about her. We burst into giggles simultaneously.

"Definitely," I agreed and rested my hand over my stomach. "You hit it right on the head, babe."

"For what it's worth, I think I'm an Annasexual," she joked and nudged me in the side.

"Beautiful, I'm flattered," I swooned, then slid closer to her. We looked at one another and laughed again. It was melodic.

"Seriously, though, *I'm* bisexual," Jamie stated with such certainty I wished I could replicate. However, she made me feel as though I didn't need to be certain about myself – because I was certain with her. "I just wanted to know about you."

"Well, as of right now, I don't know what I am. But what I do know is that I really like you a lot," I said cheekily and grazed my fingers along her knee.

"Is your dad okay with that?" she questioned and went without acknowledging my touch. Then, I knew she was slipping away again. She'd boarded the train to elsewhere.

"We don't talk about things like that. I feel weird talking to anyone about how I feel about someone else. But I don't think he'd have a problem with it. He tries to keep an open mind," I contemplated, because I'd never stressed much about the nature of what this was. It didn't dawn on me that this was a *lesbian* relationship. It was just a relationship to me, and a beautifully evolving one, at that. I didn't harp on labels and such.

"Good. I hope he likes me," Jamie contemplated with a faraway stare. She wasn't here with me, anymore.

"I know he does," I promised. His continuation of their discussions at the table were proof enough. He didn't entertain most of my friends for very long. "But what about your parents? Are they okay with it?"

"They wouldn't know, one way or the other," Jamie shrugged dismissively and cuddled up to my pillow. I wished she was cuddling up to me. "I've never been with a girl, really. I haven't dated any girls or brought home anyone that was more than a friend. I don't think they know there's anything between us."

"Do you want them to know?" I questioned and pressed my cheek against the pillow, staring at her from a better angle.

"I would like to flaunt you as my girlfriend if we ever made it official, yes," Jamie said thoughtfully. "I'm not going to hide you, or this. They'll get the hint."

As my girlfriend replayed in my mind. I loved the concept of the two of us together, officially. Having a title. Having a girlfriend.

"Okay. And they will," I nodded. "But can I ask you a question?"

"Anything, love," Jamie granted, and somehow, she was back with me. I would have whiplash if I were her, dissociating so frequently.

"How did you know – like how did you figure out what you were? I've really never even thought about it, myself," I asked her and she raised an eyebrow as she determined how to answer me.

"Well, I think the first time I realized I was attracted to girls was like – in the eighth grade," she began to reminisce.

Jamie closed in on me while discussing her journey with her sexuality. She situated herself and inched over to me in the midst of her stories. Her legs were in closer proximity and her arm was nearer, too. Her estranged yearning for me was just as present as my suppressed desire. With my encouraging *uh–huh's* and *mhm's* to let her know that I was hearing her, I slid closer – measured in centimeters. Our destination was as much the center of my bed as it was each other. Body heat was taunting us. We were near enough to feel the warmth of one another, but far enough to miss the source of it. That did not daunt me. We would be together, soon.

Much like everything else pertaining to the two of us, it was rather transient. I interrupted to suggest turning off the light, to which she permitted. After doing so, I got back into bed and we were even more approximal. Jamie was babbling, comfortably on her back and recounting her story to my ceiling. She was claiming her space, with her legs open and her arm bent behind her head – a secondary pillow. I invited myself into it by lying abreast of her. I stretched out in a similar way, and there we were: indistinctly touching. Her knee grazed mine in the air, and my arm just barely brushed her elbow. The distinct motion came when my arm listlessly settled across her abdomen. There was a pause in her reminiscence, her cognizance of what I had done so seamlessly. Acceptance followed, with her placing her hand over my arm to secure my embrace. Every other contiguous endeavor happened easily.

Jamie was enthused by her story. I was enthused by her.

I was only half–listening to her as she told me about her friend's fifteenth birthday party and the following sleepover that made her wonder. My attention was dedicated to the way my arm rose with every swell of her ribcage and fell with every slow breath she exhaled to accompany her speech. I was keen on the details of our moment, not the details of her story – although I would remember to tease her about leaving the bed because being so close to her friend made her feel "too funny." I was hearing her comical take on it now, along with the answers to the questions she'd had back then, but I was listening to the rhythms of her body more. I was as conscious of the beating in her chest and that pulsation throughout her body as I was the pace of her respiration. I felt the treble in her laugh. I was aware of the vibrations of her speech, the sound of her voice.

She was warm against me. Whenever she moved, I felt her heated skin collide with mine. I felt connected, differently.

Somehow, this was made even more intimate than our kissing. Our bodies were at different rhythms, yet we had one of our own. One that was ours to share. One that couldn't be replicated by anyone else, because they had neither the same heartbeats or breathing patterns. This moment was ours. And I lost myself in it.

Jamie

My parents weren't pleased that I'd never come home last night. Being eighteen and a legal adult and all, I didn't feel the need to inform them of my every move. I rarely told them anything at all. I left the house and walked to Small Wonder, unannounced, every day. I spent time with Anna without letting them in on our plans. I did my own thing more often than not, with no word of communication to them for anything. So why they were upset with my not coming home was beyond me.

Anna's dad dropped me off after breakfast the next morning. We'd had a good night, followed by a similar morning. It was a great memory. I felt that things had gone smoothly in the sense that I was accepted by her father. He was really the only thing that posed an obstacle to being together, and I'd passed. We'd both gotten the chance to warm up to one another at dinner, and again at breakfast. I liked him. He liked me. It boosted my spirits significantly when I went home, only to have them fall once I got inside.

I arrived around eleven, as content as could be. Anna and I could bear to be alone. We didn't have the overwhelming desire to be with one another at all hours. The time we shared was enough. I thought of it as a healthy attachment. Anna was back at home and I was resting in bed before I tackled my article for the day.

"You didn't say you'd be staying out," my mother stated distantly once I'd gotten settled back in my room. Once again, she was standing there in the doorway. Knocking was never in her plans.

"Oh, I was with Anna," I explained after looking up briefly. "I went to her house."

"Without telling anyone," she added in her usual passive–aggressive fashion.

"I didn't think I'd have to..." I replied, keeping to myself how she wouldn't have cared.

"I would like to know when my daughter isn't coming home," she said poignantly. "Sam was left here alone last night."

"Sorry," I responded out of obligation. Of course. *Sam* was the real issue, not my whereabouts.

"You've been spending a lot of time with this Anna," she lingered in the doorway, and I closed my laptop, realizing that this wasn't exactly over yet.

"Yes," I affirmed simply, giving her no details and depriving her of context.

"Who is she?" she crossed her arms curiously.

"Anna Labon," I answered. "She's a really great friend."

"And how do you know her?" she persisted.

"I met her at Small Wonder, the record store I get Corey's albums from," I sighed and succumbed to this round of twenty questions. "She works there."

"And she's the only one you've talked to after..?" my mother insinuated and inferred at once. "She's the person that gave you a reason to speak again?"

"I guess you could say that," I mumbled. That was a strange way to put it. "She's really been working towards it."

"I don't know when all of this has happened, but I'm glad for it. I'm happy you have someone, again. You were starting to scare us with all of this antisocial stuff," she shared insensitively. I thought it might've killed her to give me anything other than a backhanded compliment

"Yeah, I'm glad I met her, too..." I muttered, although I didn't feel that I was being antisocial at all. Everything I did was more than justified.

"You can bring her over as much as you'd like. I'd like to meet her one day, the right way," she said pointedly, as if I'd done her some injustice by not introducing them initially. I felt no inclination at the time and hardly did, now. "She seems like a nice girl."

"She is..." I entertained her for a few seconds more, exasperated with this conversation. This was perhaps the most extensive conversation we'd had since his accident. I didn't know why she was prolonging this.

"And I'm glad you've made a friend..." she added.

"Yeah," I looked at her blankly.

"You don't have to be so hostile," she deadpanned and gathered herself there in the doorway.

"I'm not being hostile," I glanced at her. I was being guarded. I guess she wouldn't see the difference. It was all in her perception.

"I'm only trying to talk to you," she stressed. "I haven't been able to since–"

"I don't want to talk about that," I interrupted. "Please."

"Okay," she resigned. "I would just like to talk to you. This girl has more privilege than I do, and I *live* with you."

"There's just not a lot to talk about..." I muttered. "And I'm sorry I wasn't here for Sam, but she's old enough to stay home alone anyway," I exhaled and tried to wrap up our conversation. Her estranged endeavors to relate to me were making me uncomfortable.

"You didn't tell anyone where you were," my mom entered my room with a stuttered pace. "You were out all day. The last time my child didn't come home, it was because he'd been in an accident."

"Mom," I interrupted her with my own pained speech. "*I don't want to talk about that.*"

"I worry about everyone as soon as they go out of that door. Corey, your father, your sister... You. Nothing is guaranteed. I don't want to have to worry about *something else* happening," she emphasized. "I want to know where my family is and that they are *safe*, wherever they are."

"I'm sorry," I apologized sincerely. It hadn't occurred to me that she would consider such a thing whenever I left. "I just didn't think I'd be missed."

The last part was said under my breath, but in the silence that followed my apology, it wasn't too difficult to perceive. Her expression softened. Those stern, unblinking eyes were now remorseful. She crossed my room and sat on the edge of my bed. "Jamie... Why wouldn't I miss you?"

"I really have to get this article written," I digressed and turned away from her, slightly. I made a move to open my laptop.

She placed her hand over it and prevented my progress. "Why wouldn't I miss you?" she reiterated.

"I don't know," I faltered under her intense gaze.

"Jamie," she prompted me.

"Just forget I said that," I clenched my jaw. It was getting harder to avoid her gaze. "You've proved your point, alright? I get it, I'll tell you where I'm going next time."

"Why would you ever think that?" she asked me, genuinely, one last time. She was begging for my answer with her stare, alone. I regarded her from what little distance I could maintain, and she wouldn't let me evade this. I tried, though. I looked elsewhere and avoided meeting those pleading eyes, but only lasted a few seconds.

"Because! Ever since Corey and Sam were born, I was less important. Ever since they were born, it's just automatically been my responsibility to take care of them and to look out for them. I was just a second mom, a backup you, as far as they were concerned – as far as you were concerned. I was the nanny, not their big sister. I was only seven, Mom. I was seven years old when you just forced all of that responsibility on me. It just felt like I didn't matter," I ranted and knew there were tears brimming in my eyes, but I disregarded them. If she wanted her damn answer, she would get the emotions that came with it. My voice was hoarse as my strife started to get the best of me. "It felt like I didn't matter."

In a move that didn't fit our dynamic at all, my mother wrapped her arms around me. She coaxed my head against her chest and stroked her hand along my hair. I resisted, because it was so foreign, but I relented. I let my mother hug me. I could count on my fingers how many times I'd been in this position, there against her chest. "You have always mattered, Jamie."

"In fact..." she prepared to continue. I was wetting her blouse with my tears, and remembering her perfume. "You are the glue holding this family together. I never meant to make you feel like I was putting everything on you. I've never meant to make you feel overwhelmed. Whenever I needed a helping hand, you were always right there. You've always shown that you could handle it. You've always shown that I could count on you. I am so sorry that it became a habit. I'm so sorry I've put so much on your plate."

"Jamie... My beautiful Jamie," she crooned above me and rocked my weak body. "I love you. I have always loved you. You have always been important to me, to us, my first born. Sam and Corey have their permanent places in my heart, right next to yours," she ran her hand down my back and kissed the crown of my head. "I owe you an apology for ever making you feel otherwise. And for having not expressed it enough."

I took all that she said to heart. She had no idea how much I'd needed to hear it. I tightened my grip around her aging body and nestled myself more firmly into her. "Thank you."

Our moment lasted for a few beats longer until my mother dismissed herself. She squeezed me on the shoulder, kissed my head, and let herself out of my room. I never verbalized it, but I wasn't sure how this might affect our relationship. If it did, how long? And if it didn't, what was it for? It seemed like a temporary fix, but you can't put a band–aid over years of neglect. However, I was grateful for her endeavors.

It was still fresh on my mind when I visited Anna at work, in what had become our daily routine. I recapped the entire confrontation and how abruptly it all seemed to happen. She listened to me in the same manner she always did – attentive and receptive. She listened to understand, not to respond. She never responded until I was finished. I'd always loved that about her.

"Well, I always knew that your parents loved and cared about you. But, at the same time, I'm not there, so I can't really speak on that. It makes me happy that you two had that conversation. I think you both needed it," Anna replied to my story pleasantly, leaning over the counter on her forearms.

"Yeah, we definitely did," I nodded. "It was kind of weird. She held me like she used to when I was little. You know when you're in your mom's lap and she's like, rocking you from side to side?"

"Aww, yeah," Anna related. "My mom used to sit me in her lap like that when we went to church."

"She was holding me just like that. I felt weird, but like, a good weird," I reflected. "I don't know what to think about it."

"Just take it for what it is, right now," Anna suggested. "I don't know. With the way she seems, I wouldn't get my hopes up..."

"Oh, I'm definitely not. It's probably like a once in a blue moon kind of thing. Maybe her being nicer and putting less responsibility on me will be as far as it goes, for a while," I predicted. "But in other news, she really likes you."

"It didn't even seem like she's paid attention to me, the few times I've seen her," Anna remembered and made a face to oppose my words.

"Well, she doesn't know you, but she likes you because of your influence on me. She thinks you're like, therapeutic for me or something," I laughed at how my mother perceived Anna.

"Do you?" she turned the question to me.

"I don't know. I don't think like that. Do you think you are?" I turned it right back on her.

"I wouldn't go that far. I mean, of course I think I'm helping you," Anna said after a thoughtful moment. "But we're helping each other. We're both good for each other. We're just compatible, both making each other better."

"I think you're helping me, too. But it's so weird because that's not the way you go about it. You're not like – taking pity on me or anything by hanging out with me. You don't act like I'm fragile, most of the time. You don't treat me like everyone else does. Everybody wants to help me. They say that they're helping, and they really think so, too. They force that on me. You're helping me by being my friend, first. A real friend, above everything else," I shared my disposition with her and hoped she'd agree.

"Friendship is always a good remedy," she said cheekily, then that smile dropped comedically. "Wait, did you just friendzone me? After everything we've been through?"

"Never," I smirked and grasped her chin to pull her into a kiss, to prove that our status definitely surpassed friends. "I don't do that with my friends."

"You don't have any friends," Anna said playfully, and I scoffed at her in the same fashion.

"*Your* best friend is your store manager," I returned spitefully, looking over at Cassie in the back. "You don't really have me beat."

"Whatever," Anna rolled her eyes at me and wouldn't stop her smile.

She tried to keep up her façade by biting her lip to contain her smile. I grinned widely, knowing she couldn't keep it up if I was combatting her with my own. She kinked an eyebrow and I did, too. Her lip quivered as she attempted to stand her ground, but she lost. I won a smile out of her and it was followed by a lighthearted chuckle.

"But you know, I didn't even know about you or what happened. From my point of view, I was just like why is this weirdo not speaking?" she teased me again, comfortable enough to mess with me like that consecutively now. "*That* was the real mystery."

I'd noticed the progress in our relationship when she'd affectionately called me a loser for the first time, one day in her room. In one of my less graceful moments, I'd bumped into her dresser and caused her belongings to fall off. She was sitting there on the bed, cross–legged, as I apologized and picked them up. She giggled at me and called me a loser under her breath. I was elated by it. No one deemed me secure enough to joke with like that anymore. They feared such a name would get under my skin, and they were right, but I wasn't that sensitive most times. Due to my elective mutism, I *was* weird. I *did* seem like a loser. I *did* seem crazy. And no one wanted to utter those names because it fit me too snugly. But Anna had.

I couldn't explain to her why I was smiling, so. And I didn't want to dampen the atmosphere by saying so. So I let my smile suffice and let her fallen items lay on the ground for a few minutes more as I closed in on her. We ended up kissing and tasting the laughter of one another in the midst of it. She never understood the sentiment behind my sudden giddiness, but it was one of those things she'd accepted at face value.

"I know. And you still treated me like a normal person between all of that," I acknowledged, because that was most monumental to me.

"Normal..." she persisted in this taunting mood of hers by making a face at the inference.

"Seriously, A-L," I laughed and tried to get her back on track. I was trying to share something important. "I just love that you're not on a mission of trying to fix me. It's almost as if you don't see me as broken. I'm not some project for you. You don't even try to force your help on me. I love that about you."

"Okay, okay," Anna calmed down in her funny business and prepared to give me a real response. "You've got your problems, but we all do. You're right, though. I'm not trying to fix you. I just want to be the one to be there for you. I'm glad you're letting me be that person, babe."

"You are my person," I clarified for her. Her face softened. She leaned over the counter and reached for my hand, then she grabbed the other. With both of my hands in her hold and her eyes now locked with mine, she broke into a slow smile – much different from the silly ones she'd been wearing before. It appeared that that meant something to her.

Anna managed to melt my heart with only two words of her own. "You're mine."

Jamie

Anna would get the opportunity to be there for me sooner than she thought. Corey's date was approaching, fast. We spent time together in the same way, but it weighed more on me than her. It meant more to me than it did to her. She was distracting me from needing to distract myself.

Corey was hit on July sixteenth, but he died on the nineteenth. All of the time between was fit for heartache. Corey's date wasn't a single day, it was a cluster of them – of awful, devastating days where nothing had gotten better. No news was not good news, then. We had no news, and then we got the worst news possible. The days on the calendar depressed me, because I remembered what each one had brought. Had it really been a year without him, already?

Anna noticed the shift in my behavior in the days leading up to it. I hated to say it, but even *she* wasn't enough to pull me out of what I was feeling. There was no break in this. I wanted to be alone, but didn't want to sadden her for not being enough. But she couldn't have been enough. No one posed as consolation. What I'd done had returned to the forefront of my mind, like it used to be.

The antidepressants I'd been prescribed had little effect, so I'd upped my dosage. I'd read the warning label, but felt no sense of danger or peril from the possibility of overdosing. It seemed just.

I didn't call myself suicidal. It was too clinical. Too cut and dry. Instead, I grew fond of the term: contemplative. I thought about it, often. But that's all I ever did. I only thought about it. But, on the days it was really hard, on the days where the guilt was too much, on the days where his absence really got to be debilitating, I would do a little more than think about it. I would take initiative to feel better, albeit not the safest of strategies.

On some sleepless nights, I'd swipe my mom's prescribed insomniac medicine. Combined with my own sedatives, the outcome was unpredictable. The medication I was to take to alleviate this depression had specific dosage instructions. And when it got really bad, I would use it as a scapegoat. I felt really bad, so I took an extra. A few extra. Several extra. To feel better, of course. At times, I took pills that were not mine. I was curious if the mixing of the two would be lethal. I wasn't hoping for much of anything, but I wasn't discouraging or fearing anything, either. I thought that if anything were to happen, I wouldn't have cared. Suicide is intentional. I didn't think I had those specific intentions, yet there is no word for one that doesn't care, either way.

Numb was a nice one. Empty fit well. Demoralized could do, and all of its synonyms. I was every single one.

And Anna noticed. She tried to act like she wasn't, and that nothing was out of the ordinary. But I saw her, seeing me. Seeing me change. Seeing me lose the desire to overcompensate with the smiles and giggles, being too exhausted to do so. Seeing me pull away from her and wanting to occupy my own, separate space. Seeing me come later and leave earlier. And I didn't want her to see that. I didn't want her to see it getting harder for me. I didn't want her to see what I wasn't showing her, what she could usually distract me from. What she wasn't able to do for me anymore. At least not now.

So I stopped coming. I didn't want her to bear this burden. I could get through it alone, like I had been. I didn't want to sadden her with my dissociation. I didn't want her to think that it was her fault, or that it was anything she'd done, because she had the tendency to go down that route. She wanted to be my savior and I didn't want to crush her spirit by showing her that she wasn't – not really. I didn't want her to know that her help was temporary, and that it faded with every day that crept closer. I didn't want to hurt her feelings. I didn't want to hurt her.

The first day I skipped out on stopping by, she let me evade her. The second day, I got a text and a call later on after not replying to her message. On the third day that I didn't pay her a visit, she paid me one. Anna came to my house on July seventeenth, a year and a day after Corey had been struck down.

This was the day, a year ago, that we learned he was not responding to any stimuli and that he was most likely brain–dead. His doctor informed us of the procedure to find this out and what it consisted of along with the expenses of life support, if that was the case. This was the day everything about his accident changed. Before word of that, we had so much faith. People came out of comas. People grew to own scars and recover from wounds. People had stories to tell afterwards. We'd seen the movies. We'd seen the news. It was rare, sure, but it was possible. We knew Corey was capable of miracles since his premature birth. We knew he was strong enough to make it, and we'd truly deluded ourselves into believing so. The plausibility of a vegetative state was soul–crushing and mind–numbing. Reality took no mercy on us. And it still wasn't, because we were here, one year later, to mourn Corey's death. We were here and he was not.

I was dealing with that knowledge on my own when my mom called up the stairs that Anna was here. I hadn't been doing anything, save sitting on his bed. My eyes had been trained on the collection of albums he'd never gotten to build for himself, what I had taken over. They were organized in the case I'd gotten him. His collection was filling in nicely. He'd once described to me that he wanted two shelves full of CDs with a boombox in the middle to play them on. I was still working on completing his first shelf, but I planned on investing in his boombox soon. Maybe then, I'll spend my money elsewhere – on me again.

 I got the idea to do this shortly after his funeral. Initially, I never wanted to set foot in Small Wonder ever again. I never wanted to go to that plaza for anything. It had been much too hard. But one day, after reminiscing on the real reason he'd passed, I made the trip. I started with the same album he'd begged me for: Coldplay's *A Head Full of Dreams*. I bought that for him and it alleviated some of the guilt, but just barely. I felt inclined to buy him another one, the next day. And another the next day. With school, I went when I could. It wasn't a daily mission I took on, and I stopped doing it for a while because I needed to focus on senior year. When the summer came again, I started the practice back up. The house was too quiet without him. I needed to get out. And that's how all of this began again.

 I reflected on all of it as I sat, starting at his wall. I remembered his logic behind the shade of his walls. Blue was too typical of a color for a boy's room. But he didn't like green. So he chose charcoal grey, because it was cool. No one opposed to it verbally, but we all thought that a grey room would be kind of dreary. No one could discourage him, anyway, because he'd given it so much thought. Corey's vision of décor was... Interesting, to say the least. He found such fascination in things before his time. The nineties was his favorite era, and he playfully held a grudge against my parents for having him near the 2000's. He'd gone through our garage in search of storage boxes of old things. He'd hung up some cassette tapes on his walls for reasons unbeknownst to anyone else. He'd taped our dad's old license plates above the frame of his bed. He'd found a way to string four vinyl records up along his wall, framing his window. He didn't have any pictures or posters or anything normal in his room, except for the Falcons poster on his door. My little brother was so strange. I missed him. But I found a solace in being in his room, sometimes.

"Jamie?" my mom called me again. "Anna's coming up!"

"Yeah," I acknowledged her. Lethargically, I pushed myself off of his bed. I heard Anna approaching, and I knew she was headed for my room. I turned Corey's doorknob and cracked the door open just in time to see her on her way there.

"Oh, hi," she faltered in her steps when I emerged. She broke into a smile that I didn't return.

"Hey," I greeted her, although I didn't want to see her.

"Um," Anna said, just to say something. I was already tired. "I don't have to stay or anything, but I just wanted to check on you... Make sure you're okay..." she said quietly and manipulated her fingers. "*Are* you okay?"

"Yeah," I nodded and shifted my eyes to the ground. I didn't want to come off as standoffish as I was, but I really wasn't in the mood. For anything.

"It's just, I haven't seen you in a few days, now. It was just kinda – I don't know. You were coming every day and staying all day and then you just–"

"I said I'm okay, Anna," I stressed to her and was already exasperated with her company. I wasn't seeing her for a reason. I didn't want to be around.

"Oh," she accepted my obvious lie. I saw her trying to assess me, trying to see whether this was a case she should push or not. Thankfully, she let it go. "Okay."

"Sorry, I don't mean to snap at you," I apologized and ran my hands over my face, because it really wasn't her fault. She didn't deserve this treatment.

"It's okay," she granted and fell into step as I trudged to my room.

I almost didn't want her to follow me. I didn't want to be around her at all and I felt awful for it. I stood in the doorway and held up my hand to stall her advances. "Anna..."

"I didn't – Uh, I didn't do anything... Right?" she knitted her brow, seemingly terrified of the possibility. As if it could even be a possibility.

"No, you didn't. You never do," I appeased her. "You're fine. I'm just not the best company to keep right now, so..."

"Do you wanna talk about it?" she offered and tried to be closer by reaching for my hand. "I don't mind–"

"No," I stated resolutely and evaded her touch. I was trying to get my point across without being rude to her, because she was the last person I'd want to be nasty towards.

"But you usually would?" she reminded me. "Whatever's bothering you has been bothering you for the past few days, now... And you would at least let me be around..."

"Can't I have some time to myself?" I scoffed at her perception, although she didn't mean it like that. I didn't mean it like that, either.

"Of course you can, but it's just kind of weird how you are. This is isolation. I don't need to be with you at all hours of the day or anything, but I'd like to know that you're fine, wherever you are... You didn't answer my texts and you sounded really weird on the phone. I just wanted to make sure you were okay, babe," Anna elaborated without looking away.

"You sound like my mom," I wrote her off, finally. This was the forced help. She was doing it.

"I'm not trying to. I just – I care about you. And you've just pulled away from everything. Completely. I was worried about you, Jamie..." Anna pressed on, and I didn't want to hear it.

"Well, don't worry. I told you I was okay," I told her and pursed my lips.

Anna stared at me for a minute, then. A solid minute of her searching my eyes. And when I looked away, I felt her gaze linger. Too long. What the hell was she looking at?

"What is wrong with you?" she begged of me.

"What's wrong with *you*? I just fucking told you I was okay and you're still here. What do you want?" I retorted in a manner much too vile for her. I didn't treat Anna this way. I never did. I didn't want to start now. "Sorry. You know what – You should go."

Anna looked wounded by what I'd said. I had never spoken to her like that before. And I never wanted to see that defeated expression again. "I just want you to talk to me."

"I don't need to talk to anyone," I continued, despite how I was actively hurting her feelings. Perhaps that was what I needed to do to get her to go on. "Can you just–"

"Was it today?" she interrupted me intuitively, then she looked to my calendar. "Is that why you're – Is today the day it happ–"

"No, it wasn't *today*. It's none of your business," I grimaced at how she was trying to bring herself into this. She didn't belong in it. She didn't belong here.

"You told me it was the nineteenth," Anna remembered. "But today is only the seventeenth... What happened today?"

"Nothing," I dismissed her endeavors.

"Why are you shutting me out?" Anna almost whined as her shoulders slumped. "You know I'm the one person you can talk to about anything, Jamie."

"I can talk to you about anything when I fucking come to you, *wanting* to talk about it. Not when you come here, forcing it out of me. I want to be left alone," I said through tight lips.

"Please let me be there for you. Here I am. I... I'm *here*," Anna stressed to me, but I couldn't. "Just – Just let me–"

"I don't want you here," I deadpanned and took a seat on my bed, with my back to her.

"Jamie," Anna pleaded for my attention.

"Can you just leave?" I asked of her over my shoulder.

"You don't mean that," Anna stood there defiantly. "What happened? What changed?"

"I don't want you here," I repeated solemnly. Corey was weighing on me more than usual. I was volatile and I didn't want her to catch the tail end of something that had nothing to do with her.

"I'm not gonna be like your other friends that let you push them away. I'm not budging, Jamie. I don't want you to go through this alone, I care about you. Let me show you," Anna blatantly ignored my request and came to my bedside. She placed her hand on my shoulder. And I lost it.

"Anna, go away. I don't fucking want you here. You think you can just fucking show up and everything is better. It's not better. It never fucking gets better. I feel like this all the fucking time and I don't know what to do. And you can't help me. Just leave. Get out of here. I can take care of myself. I have been," I spat venom at her and lost my composure at once. This crossfire reminded me of my last words to Corey. It was too much. "You're acting just like everybody else. You push too hard, and I don't want to be pushed. God, leave me alone when I tell you to leave me alone."

"I'm not leaving you alone," Anna defied me, but stepped back, giving me a sliver of what I wanted. I wanted complete solitude to feel this on my own. "You've convinced yourself that that's what you want, just because that's all you're used to. You don't have to do that anymore. I am right here."

I clenched my jaw in response. Clearly, she wasn't going to abide by my wishes. As I thought about it, I didn't even know if I truly wanted her to go. It was easiest. I didn't want to have to explain. I didn't want to have to express. I didn't want her to see the kind of state I could fall into. I wanted her perception of me to stay as lighthearted as it had been, before.

I wanted that version of me to remain in her mind, not the one I succumbed to when I returned home. Not the one I was whenever she wasn't here, before I'd met her.

"Jamie, I'm right here. Please?" Anna requested with a softer approach.

But she was begging for me to let her in. It reminded me of the way she'd begged for me to speak to her for the first time. Now I had too much to say and I didn't want to overwhelm her, or myself by verbalizing it. I clenched my jaw again and took a quick, regretful look at her. "Today's the day he went brain–dead."

"Oh, God... I'm sorry," she mumbled, and there it was: the reason I hardly articulated anything regarding it. I hated the sympathetic *I'm sorry* that comes with the sharing of bad news. It irked me because no one can gauge the toll it takes, but they say that they are sorry – as if they had anything to do with it. It was a safe, detached reply. But what the hell were you supposed to say, anyway? Everyone wants you to talk about it. They say that you can talk to them. I avoided talking about it, because I was the only one doing the talking. It was not a conversation, it was a monologue. The spotlight was on me. And I never wanted it to be.

"Just a day later?" she inferred.

I grimly nodded in slow affirmation. "Every day from his accident to him actually–" I exhaled sharply. "Actually dying were the worst of my life."

"I can imagine how hard that must've been," Anna tried to relate, but she couldn't. There was no way she could've. And it pissed me off.

"No, you can't," I cut my eyes towards her. "You don't have any idea what it was like," I finally choked out to her and my stomach lurched uncomfortably. I didn't want to feel this.

The stone–cold façade was over. My resolve crumbled just as Anna tried to recover from her lapse.

"Well, no, I didn't mean–" Anna tried to take back her words, but I interrupted her bitterly.

"They told us he was dead. They *told* us. But my mom wouldn't believe them, because his heart was still beating. But it wasn't him – It was the damn machine... His heart was beating because of a *machine*, Anna. He couldn't have done it by himself. He was already dead. Corey... Corey was already dead, because of me–"

"It isn't your fault," Anna preached her mantra with misty eyes.

"My dad was the one that told them to take him off of life support. We couldn't fucking afford it. It cost thousands of dollars, every day. Every second was costing us. By the third day with no progress, we just had to let him go. My mom hated my dad for it. She didn't speak to him for months, Anna. She blames him for killing Corey, but she should be blaming me. It *is* my fault. It's all my fault. I killed him," I announced wretchedly and bowed over on my bed, letting that dissociation absolve into guilt again. My hands were shaking as I tried to cover my face and shield my tears. In trying to contain my emotion, I was steadily losing ground. My lip was trembling and my chest was heaving, all in front of Anna.

"Jamie, you did not–" she tried once more, but I was beyond that.

"And I let my dad take the blame for what I did!" I leaned up to stress to her. "He was doing what was best for all of us. He couldn't let us go broke, trying to keep Corey alive when he was dead, anyway. And we get that, but it was just so..." I trailed off and attempted to clear away the thickness in my throat. "It was just so fucking hard."

"I just remember holding his hand and it was still warm. It was *still warm*, like he was alive. But it wasn't real. He was kept warm because of an IV, because of the blankets – not because he was alive. And I could feel his pulse through his hand, but that wasn't real either. The machine he was hooked up to was simulating a heartbeat and his breathing and... Fucking everything that makes you alive. If we took him off of it, he would die. And that's exactly what happened..."

"He looked so little, surrounded by all of that stuff. My little brother... And I took him for granted every day. He was annoying, but he was still my little brother. And I love him so much. And I'm so shitty because I never really told him that. I was always yelling at him and telling him to leave me alone and making fun of him.... Anna, the last thing I ever said to him, I was yelling at him. I was the one being a bitch. I was the one that wouldn't give up money that I had, and I turned it on him and made it his problem for being needy and for begging and for not having money, himself. He was fucking fourteen, how was he supposed to have his own money? How could I fucking do that? How could I treat him that way? I didn't even deserve him," I reflected and my speech was nearly incoherent. I was blubbering and sniffling and crying and Anna was a trooper for sitting there through it all.

She sat through my crying spell and didn't intervene after a while. I realized that I'd pegged her all wrong. She didn't force anything at all. She didn't throw her arms around me and she didn't demand comfort. She didn't say much of anything or give me advice as much as she sat there, listening to me – taking everything in. The only thing she ever forced me to do was to acknowledge that she cared about me, and to understand that I could confide in her without judgement.

"He died because of eleven dollars," I gave a blunt synopsis after I'd wiped my face and sat up straight once more. "And I have to live with that."

"No, it was because of a drunk driver. Because the police didn't catch him in time. He died because that man was drinking and driving, and *speeding*, not because you didn't give him the money," she swore adamantly.

"He wouldn't have been if it weren't for me," I reminded her tersely.

"How do you know that? How do you know that even if you had given him the money, you wouldn't have left the store at the same time? That you wouldn't have been crossing the street at the same time he was coming, anyway?"

"I don't, but maybe at least then I could've been there to save him or warn him or something..." I assumed, but then thought that I was overestimating my charity. "Or I could've been hit instead."

"And what if you couldn't?" Anna proposed to me, staring at me intently.

"Then..." I trailed and really considered what she was saying.

"I know we're not really big on religion, so I'll speak in terms of the universe, like you said to me that day at the park, on the bench. Things happen for a reason. I'm not saying that it's always for a good reason, but they do. I'm not gonna blow up my self importance and say he left you so I could find you, but isn't that how you thought about it at one point?"

"Yeah, I guess," I mumbled. I'd considered the balance of it all.

"Well then continue to think that way, if it helps. As always, you can tell me if I'm overstepping... But I can't help thinking that maybe this would've happened, regardless of if you gave him those couple of dollars. The universe doesn't do anything on accident. It can be unfortunate, but there are no mistakes. That car would've found Corey anyway. Maybe not that day, but eventually. You lose people when they're young, and it sucks, but there's nothing you could've done. There's nothing you can do, now. You're not getting anywhere by blaming yourself. It's only destroying you."

"You can't understand what it's like to lose your brother at your own hands. I think about him every single day, Anna. He could've still been here if it wasn't for my selfishness... I killed Corey and–"

"I don't ever want to hear you say that again. You didn't kill anyone. *You are not a murderer*," Anna grabbed me by the shoulders and stressed it to me. "Sure, if you want to say that you played a role in it, then you did. You could've given him the money, but you didn't. And he would've been mad at you, but guess what? He would've survived that. That isn't what killed him, Jamie. You aren't the one that struck him down with that car. You weren't behind the wheel. That man was, and that man killed your brother. *Not you*."

"I guess that makes sense, but–" I weighed her admission internally, but it didn't lessen the guilt I felt.

"There is no *but*, babe. It wasn't your fault and you can't keep beating yourself up for it. I can't watch you do this to yourself anymore. You have to let that part of the angst go. You have to let that guilt go," Anna let her arms fall away, letting her hand graze my arm as they did.

"I just don't know if I can," I mumbled, because things were never that easy. Her uncomplicated way of thinking and pattern of life wouldn't allow her to comprehend this.

However, she did shed light on a new perspective. I'd never once considered that Corey's fate was predetermined. Maye that car *would've* found him anyway. Maybe he was *supposed* to be taken from me. I'd spent so much time wallowing – drowning – in this guilt that I'd never allowed anything else to be. The thought that the events could be tweaked to collide with us, regardless, had never occurred to me.

What if I *wasn't* the sole cause of it?

Corey could've ben coming out of Small Wonder at the same time the car was coming, anyway. What if I had given him the money, and treated him to a snack afterwards? Who knows? I didn't, and I couldn't. In the smallest increment, I felt it free my conscience.

"Maybe you will one day," she quoted me. "You owe it to yourself."

"I think I owe it to you, too," I concluded. She'd just introduced me to an entirely new way of thinking.

"Don't think like that. It's not for me, you deserve peace for yourself–" Anna readily began her tangent.

"I mean that you just kinda made me realize something... I owe the revelation to you," I clarified.

"What'd you realize?" Anna leaned back to assess me.

"That maybe it's not all on me... Not 100%. I mean, I definitely had a big part in it, but like, there were more important things that had to happen in order for his accident to happen."

"Exactly. You're just a small part of it. Otherwise, it would've been just like all the other times you were being a bratty big sister and he was being the annoying, needy little brother. Your every day dynamic. No offense," Anna smirked.

"None taken," I almost laughed.

"I'm glad I could finally make you understand that, a little," Anna grinned to me, exuding pride.

"Me, too," I seconded and leaned into her, thanking her for her stubborn presence. Anna brought her arm over me and said nothing. I appreciated her. Immensely.

I only nodded and leaned into her, allowing myself to be comforted. Anna let me sit there without butchering the silence. I felt that maybe I should've apologized to her for my snark and snappiness, but also assumed that she knew it wasn't towards her. None of it was directed at her.

"Thanks," I said simply and let it suffice. It was loaded with sentiment.

"Always," Anna rubbed my shoulder, and I knew she understood everything I wanted to communicate.

"Did you walk here?" I raised my head slightly to ask.

"I did," she affirmed. "I went through the shortcut and all."

"Well, then you probably worked up an appetite," I assumed. "Are you hungry?"

"A little bit," Anna agreed. "But you know I never turn down a snack."

"I think I'll treat you for being so great to me all the time. I have no idea what we have downstairs, but I'll put together something for you," I announced and stood up.

"You cook?" Anna asked in pleasant surprise.

"I can follow a recipe, yes," I answered with a smirk.

"Oh, man..." Anna jokingly second–guessed her decision.

"Let me go clean myself up," I mentioned just before going across the hall to the bathroom. I felt kind of gross, sitting there in the aftermath of that anguish. My face felt puffy and I knew my eyes were red. It was nothing a little cold water couldn't fix. I excused myself and left Anna there on my bed.

When I returned, she was hovering over my dresser. It didn't strike me as anything out of the ordinary. Anna liked to fiddle with my things often. But when I walked back in, she seemed startled by my presence.

"You okay?" I asked in the process of further drying my hands on my pants.

"Uh – Are all of these yours?" she asked uncertainly, standing just in front of my dresser.

When I approached to see what she was talking about, I froze. She was staring at the several pill bottles I'd collected from around the house. My mom's, my dad's, mine. We all had our issues.

"Um–" I stalled and tried to gather my thoughts. I didn't want to freak her out. "No, but–"

"What are these for?" Anna asked a little too cautiously for my liking. I didn't like the way she was scrutinizing them, or me.

"I mean, I've got some stuff going on... I take medicine..." I answered her, trying not to be outwardly defensive. "You know that..."

"Jamie, this is Xanax," Anna said alarmingly, as if I was using it for recreational use. Had she forgotten the medicinal uses for it? What it was intended for?

"And it's prescribed," I commented as I snatched it away from her. "I'm not doing drugs. I have anxiety, amongst other things. You don't know everything about me, alright?"

"So, you mean to tell me that you're taking all of these?"

"I said they weren't all mine. But most of them are," I shrugged and tried to belittle the pill bottles to the best of my abilities. I also didn't answer her question. The answer had been yes.

"Then why do you have medicine that isn't yours?" she further interrogated me. "I don't even know what half of this stuff is..."

"Sleeping pills... Antidepressants... Pain relievers..." I listed blankly. "What?"

"That's a lot..." Anna looked at them all uncomfortably.

"I have a lot going on," I explained tersely. "You take medicine you're not prescribed sometimes, don't you? You don't have a prescription for fucking Ibuprofen, do you? Calm down, A-L."

"Yeah, but I'm also not taking anything regularly... I just don't think it's a good idea to be mixing all of this stuff without knowing what you're doing... What if something happened?" Anna reasoned innocently, and I was trying my best to be impassive about it all. I pursed my lips and looked down at my feet, because it was too demanding to meet her eyes. She didn't seem to be thinking that way, and I was grateful. I didn't want her in on that at all. I didn't want to have that conversation.

"I guess I've just been a little careless," I muttered more so to myself than to her, grimacing at the way I'd left them out. I looked up at her and tried to downplay it. "It's fine," I offered a halfhearted laugh in light of it.

But I suppose I'd never been good at my poker face.

"Unless... You *do* know what you're doing..." Anna's brow lowered as she gazed at me, then to those damned pills.

"What are you trying to say?" I clenched my jaw uncomfortably.

"What are you trying to do?" she asked me a question of her own, and her voice cracked in asking it. I felt sick when I noticed those precious tears of hers brimming in her eyes. "Jamie..."

"Stop saying my name like that," I mumbled through my strife. I swallowed harshly and refused to look at her.

"What are you trying to do?" she repeated and gathered all of them. The way they all rattled within her hands made my heart plunge. I didn't want to know what she was thinking. And I wasn't going to validate it. I couldn't, not with Anna looking at me like that. Not with Anna here, with her tears now falling. Not with Anna caring this much about me. In that moment, I knew that I *did* care what became of me. I did care.

"I'm..." I paused and chose my words very carefully. "I'm trying to get through it," I managed to say after clearing my throat.

Anna slowly put them back where she found them and wiped her eyes. And I knew she knew. "Jamie, people care about you."

"I know that," I answered heavily. "Can we just go downstairs?"

"I've lost my appetite," Anna declined lowly, hugging her arms against her chest.

"Christ, Anna..." I exhaled a labored breath. "Well, I need some water."

I brushed past her on my way out and tried to compose myself by taking a deep breath. I didn't want Anna worrying about me needlessly. I wasn't going to do it. I wouldn't. Especially not now. I reached into the refrigerator and got two bottles of water. When I got back into my room, Anna was the one looking detached.

"Here, babe," I offered her the bottle of water and took my seat on the bed next to her.

"Thanks," she took it and set it aside.

"So... Um – How was work?" I tried my hand at distraction.

"It was fine," Anna entertained me distantly. "The usual."

"Anna," I called in exasperation when I saw that I couldn't evade the explanation.

"Yeah?" she replied despondently.

"I was never *actually* going to do it," I announced and picked up her hand. "With the pills... I was never... *Trying*..."

"So that is why you had them?" Anna retracted her hand and refused to look at me. I refused to confirm that. "I thought that maybe I was overreacting..."

"Look at me," I asked of her, because this warranted eye contact. I understood her anger and disappointment, but this was the only disposition she needed to be focusing on. And when she looked at me, I felt as if I was miles away from her. "Anna, I wouldn't do that."

"Why would you even put yourself in the position for something to happen..." Anna's voice went hoarse again and she shifted her gaze away from me once more.

"Because I didn't care. I'm selfish sometimes. I only think of how I'm feeling. And all I know is that when I'm feeling like that, I don't want to feel it anymore. So – Yes, I've taken medicine that wasn't mine. I'm trying to cope. I wasn't trying to do.... *That*... But... I... I wasn't opposed to it happening, either," I admitted, and probably shouldn't have. Anna reacted strongly to that. She pulled away from me and bowed her head, letting out what I hoped wasn't a sob. I didn't want to make her cry anymore.

"But – But I'm speaking in past tense. I wouldn't, now. I wouldn't at all," I tried to promise.

"But you wanted to," Anna said regretfully. "You took them because some part of you wanted to. I can't–"

"Anna, I didn't. I was taking them for real reasons. I had some insomnia going on and I–"

"Something could've happened to you," she interrupted me bitterly.

"I promise. I'm fucked up, but... I wouldn't do that. I know what death can do to people. I know how differently people react. I can't do that to anyone else, ever again. I can't do that to my parents, twice. I can't do that to you."

"It's not about me, Jamie. You should want to be here for yourself. Stop basing your decisions on me. Put yourself first. Jesus, that's what you don't understand. I'm not worried about you because of how it would affect me. I worry because you don't care enough about yourself. You come before anyone else, period. And it's almost like you don't know that. Or if you know it, you don't believe it. That's what breaks my heart," Anna succumbed to her sadness and let her tears fall.

"I've always struggled with that, but I'm working on it. You just don't understand how important you are to me. I do all these things for you because I feel like that's what I owe you," I struggled to explain myself, but there was no way she could understand my compulsion.

"You don't owe me anything. I keep telling you that," Anna grimaced.

"Well, I need to tell you something," I retorted, then battled with myself on sharing the details. I wanted to take it back as soon as I said it, because now I had to continue. "The day we met – Or – When you started talking to me... I... I was thinking about it..."

"Jamie..." Anna shook her head and tried to save herself from what I would say.

"And then you said hi to me – Really said hi to me, not the usual customer employee interaction..." I remembered.

"Yeah... So?" Anna trailed expectantly. "You still don't owe me anything just for being nice to you."

"So... Before that, I was always thinking of how I'd lost all of my friends and pushed them away, and my family life was awful, and no one was there for me, and no one really cared about me, and it wouldn't really matter if I was gone... I don't want to tell you how drastically I was thinking about it, but I just really felt like I could disappear and it wouldn't disrupt anything. Back then, I wanted to. It was bad, then..." I forced myself to continue. "You noticed me when I felt most invisible. You don't know how much that meant to me."

"And you didn't... Because I talked to you?" Anna's eyes glossed over.

"I mean – I wouldn't have, really... But I would always want to... I used to think about it... Way too often," I bared my secrets.

Anna's teary eyes discreetly fell to my arms, assessing my forearms. I knew she was looking for scars, but there were none. I didn't turn to self–harming. It didn't appeal to me.

"I never did that, either," I addressed her gaze. "I didn't want to draw attention to myself. I didn't want someone to notice and try to get me counseling and a therapist and shit.

So, I didn't. I never did anything about my thoughts. I just sat there and thought them."

"That might be a part of the problem," Anna said, and there was no spite in her comment.

"Yeah, it might be..." I was willing to acknowledge. "But what I'm saying is, you don't have to worry about that. Thinking about something doesn't have to mean you'll do something about it. And usually now, I'm not thinking of anything like that. Now, I think of you. I always think of you."

"I may not think of myself first, but you're teaching me how to. My perception of myself has always been so shitty, but you came along and made me think that I might've actually been worth something. You're changing me in ways you don't even know, and in ways you can't see. My mom has noticed, and she knows it's because of you. I have everything to thank you for, Anna. You don't have any idea what you've done for me," I articulated now that I had her attention. "What you're still doing for me."

"Come here," Anna extended her arms towards me, inviting me into her hold. She embraced me and nestled her chin into my neck.

"I love you," I announced without the fanfare of saying it for the first time. We'd surpassed that. It was obvious. She had to know, much like I knew she loved me. Though I couldn't place to what extent just yet, we shared a connection to prove the fact regardless. "And I would never do that to you. You have my word."

"I love you," Anna hung in the moment and looked up at me. That was as big as our fanfare got, that mutual understanding through eye contact. It was followed by a smile, a bashful one. I ended up smiling, myself, because she was cute. "And I believe you."

"Well, okay," I said dumbly, with nothing more to profess.

"Okay," Anna replied just as listlessly. "Well – Can I say one more thing?"

"Of course," I granted.

"You deserve good things," she said and traced the outline of my knuckles. "And I want to be one of them."

"You are one of them," I replied softly. "You're most of them."

"No – I mean – What I mean is... I want to be your girlfriend, Jamie," Anna clarified and threw me for a loop. "I guess that wasn't as clear as it should've been."

I was rendered speechless by the proposal. It seemed out of place. Was that out of pity? I didn't want her to regret it later, just because we were caught in the moment now. "Are you sure?"

"Am I sure..." she mocked me. "I want this – like – I have always wanted this. I want to be here for you. I want the crying and pouring our hearts out and laughing, five minutes later. I want the kissing and the cuddling and I want it to mean something. I want the security of knowing that it means something to both of us. I want that as your girlfriend. I like you so much, and I love you on top of that. This just makes me want it more. I want you to be my girlfriend. I want to be yours."

"I've always told you that I'm yours," I leaned forward and kissed her forehead. "Remember? The first time we kissed, that was exactly what I told you. And I meant it, Anna. But I didn't know if you *could* be mine. I didn't know if you could handle... Me. I didn't know if you could deal with all of my fucking baggage and I didn't want you to. I was trying to protect you, or something. Maybe I was trying to protect myself, but the more I wanted you, the more I wanted distance from you. I couldn't risk dimming your light. But all the time, you're letting me borrow some. And what I thought would happen, isn't happening. I'm better now because I've met you, because I have you," I gave an extremely longwinded response, only to say one thing. "And now you have me, too. I would love to be your girlfriend."

"Yeah?" Anna confirmed as a slow, incredulous smile spread across her precious face.

"Yeah," I grinned in awe of how this all ended up. Our conversations had taken so many twists and turns since she'd showed up. Surprisingly, none of it ended in anyone storming out. We were just as good, possibly better, than we had been. As two smiling fools, we leaned in simultaneously to seal the deal with a kiss.

Jamie

The rest of the summer evolved beautifully after we'd made things official. Since that revelation Anna provided me, I was determined to go about my life differently. Corey's date came and went, and Anna was there by my side without question. It wasn't as debilitating as I'd prepared myself for. Her perception lingered in my mind, that it wasn't ultimately my fault. That recurring mantra alleviated a lot of the stress that came with it. That day was spent flipping through photo albums, filled with baby pictures from our youth. The atmosphere shifted when we began focusing on mine, specifically. Anna was so tickled and enamored with the pictures from my childhood. She'd taken my mind off of it and kept me distracted when we went back to Cold Stone. His date, what I thought would be an impossible day to survive, ended on a positive note – giggling with Anna in an ice cream parlor.

I wore a smile as I thought about it on my way to Small Wonder. I was content. I felt no heaviness whatsoever and it was a feeling I'd been getting used to lately.

I hadn't been genuinely happy in a long time, I couldn't find it in me after the accident. I was getting by, day by day. Everything was a routine blur, just going through the motions. With Corey's accident happening the summer before my senior year, it tainted my experiences significantly. I opted out of participating in most activities. My friendships began to wane. I digressed from all clubs and sports I'd been dying to dominate as the top of my class. I didn't attend homecoming, or even prom. I had no interest in our senior trip. I only did the bare minimum to pass my classes. I was surprised I'd managed to graduate at the rate I was going.

It was my own fault, I'd isolated myself. My reaction to Corey's death was extremely unhealthy. It was self–destructive. Anna, tentatively wielding her hammer, fixed me. Before her, I was veritably swimming in a state of near depression. I wasn't happy. I was getting by in silence. When I met her, all of that changed. She provided attention, understanding, happiness, and affection. She provided my sunset.

Long before we were dating, she could make my day just by smiling at me. I longed to get back to Small Wonder the next day, just so I could see her flustered state all over again. She was my favorite part of my routine. Her presence was a solace to me. I didn't want to disappear. I didn't want to join Corey out of guilt, I wanted to live just to see her. Self loathing and self depreciation didn't consume my thoughts, she did.

Slowly, but surely, she's helped me recover from the accident. There has been progress, every single day. With every smile, she's effortlessly scaled the walls I've built up over time. With each hug, she's helped me open my eyes, eyes that have been clouded by immense guilt. With each conversation, she's brought me back to a state of reality rather than my twisted, torturous perception of how my life should be. She's helped me overcome it and the burden I've been carrying for so long. She helped me realize that I was not at fault. She helped me realize that I couldn't change the unfortunate event. With her help, I've learned to accept what happened. I've learned how to begin moving on.

It was just in time, too. School was creeping up on us. I refused to have a repeat of my senior year, especially with as big of an adjustment as my freshman year in college. Anna had arrived exactly when I needed her in my life. We were preparing for my first year in college and Anna's senior year in high school, but it didn't mean anything. I was only going to a community college relatively close to home. I wasn't going away or living on campus anywhere. No one thought that would be in my best interest. Community college was a safe decision. It didn't daunt Anna and I in the slightest, although there would have to be some adjustments to her work schedule. I'd stopped going to Small Wonder as much, anyway.

I've stopped buying the albums. I've made up for my grave mistake. Spending money, simply out of guilt, wasn't healthy either. I'd indulged on what had given me relief. I'd been paying my respects, literally, for far too long. She'd helped me see that, too. Anna was easily the best thing that had happened to me. Nothing post–accident was particularly desirable until I met her. She was this window of endless possibility. I found love with her. Happiness was inevitable with Anna. I was approaching the source whilst putting all of that into perspective. When I opened the door to Small Wonder, I was met with that brilliant smile.

"I have a surprise for you," Anna beamed at me when I sauntered into Small Wonder. These days, I was really just paying my girlfriend a visit.

"I love surprises," I replied happily and kissed her when I'd made my way up to the counter. "What is it?"

"Wait here," Anna instructed me with a solitary finger. She disappeared behind the doorway and I heard her speaking to Cassie. There was some bumping and grunting, and then they emerged with a large box wrapped in Christmas paper. It was August.

"What is this?" I giggled when she and Cassie finally set it up on the counter. I hadn't asked Anna for anything and hadn't mentioned wanting anything lately. The contents of this box was beyond me.

"An early Christmas present, obviously," Anna answered sardonically with her hands on her hips. "Open it, baby."

I was overcome with giddiness as I considered it. Anna was watching me with such infectious excitement. Whatever it was, Cassie was in on it, too. I quickly stripped it of its wrapping and revealed Anna's present. My mouth was agape when an awestruck hand came to cover it. "Anna–"

"What do you think?" she clasped her hands together excitedly.

As I stared at the brand new boombox before me, I didn't know what to feel. It was a relatively large one, or maybe the box it was in was making it seem so. The picture depicted on the box was of a black stereo boombox with silver accents. The speakers were massive and I could only imagine the volume they reached. There were so many multicolored buttons and switches and nozzles on the front to toggle sound, although I wouldn't have a clue what to do with them. Complete with a CD drive, cassette tape player, radio, *and* Bluetooth, I was amazed. It had an antenna sticking up from the back and it really sold the image. It was vintage and modern at once. He would've loved it.

"Babe," I began, but was truly in awe of what she had done for us. "A-L, oh my God."

"Cassie saw it in a catalogue," Anna gestured back to her with a toothy grin as she came around the counter. "She pointed it out and I was just like – I have to get it. I remembered what you said about Corey's room and how it wouldn't be complete until he had the boombox in the middle. And – I don't know, I figured that maybe I could help out. What do you think? Do you like it?"

"I love it," I stressed to her and threw my arms around her at once. "God, I love it. I love you. Thank you."

"I thought he might like it," Anna continued in the midst of my tight hug. "You're welcome."

"I can't believe you did this," I marveled at her when I pulled away.

"I wanted to help Corey," Anna shrugged off her selfless act. "And I also wanted to see that gorgeous smile when you opened it. So, I'm pretty pleased."

"Thank you. I love it," I reiterated and hugged her again. "I'm sure he loves it, too."

"Oh yeah, check what else is inside," Anna pointed to the box with even more excitement.

"There's more?" I asked her incredulously. Anna only nodded and tried to contain herself. I opened the box, only to reveal Sara Bareilles' *Careful Confessions.* I instantly grasped the sentiment. "Wow, A-L. I don't know what to say."

"That one's not necessarily for Corey. That one is from me to you," Anna grew bashful as she explained.

"You're unbelievable," I shook my head and pulled her into me again. I kissed her once and then again on the cheek.

"Hook it up, hook it up," Cassie chimed in from the side.

"Yeah, let's give it a listen," Anna encouraged me and hung around my side. She loosely brought her arms together around my neck.

"Okay," I granted. We all worked together to bring it to life. I opened my new CD as Anna and Cassie took on the boombox. When it was all plugged in, I set *Careful Confessions* inside and Anna pressed play.

We all listened to the tracks and talked lightly amongst ourselves. Corey's boombox had amazing sound. I was grateful that they didn't have any customers walking in, interrupting our moment. We all surrounded the counter throughout the duration of the entire album. When *My Love* began, I extended my hand for Anna to take.

Although the pronouns could use some adjusting, it was almost as if Sara Bareilles had written this song specifically for she and I. I brought Anna's soft hand into my gentle hold as I held her body similarly. My other hand was settled on her lower back and hers had found its way around my waist. Together, we swayed as Sara serenaded us. Anna rested her head against my shoulder and stepped closer to me. We dropped our hands and merely held each other. I hugged her and maintained it as we rocked from side to side. Slowly, Small Wonder faded away. Anna was the only one within this moment with me. I loved her. I was happy. This was serenity.

During the bridge, I spun her around. We were going to get dizzy, but we kept on spinning. We were laughing at one another and terribly off beat, but we were happy. So happy.

"Now dip!" Anna squealed when we stopped spinning. I was dizzy and hesitant, but I went down with her, trusting her to support me. It was an easy decision. Anna dipped me and brought me back up to her mouth in the smoothest motion I'd ever experienced. She kissed me slowly and then we were standing upright. Kissing. Enjoying. Loving.

"I just love you," she told me sweetly, for my ears only.

"*I* do," I seconded in the same daze I always fell into when she kissed me like that.

The jingling of the door roused us from our mutual trance. A customer wandered in and I knew she'd have to go tend to them. Anna didn't let me go, though. I loved that she was not ashamed to be with me, no matter whose scrutiny we were under. She kissed my cheek and let her arms fall away begrudgingly when they drew nearer. "Give me a minute."

Following that intrusion, we didn't really try to have time to ourselves. I stayed at a safe distance long enough for her to do her job. It was Saturday and their busiest day. I knew that. I didn't mind it. I observed from the far end of the counter and waited for my girlfriend to finish her shift.

Because of the boombox's size and weight, I didn't try to take it back home on my own. I asked my parents to pick it up for me, along with Anna and I. They came to get us soon enough. Anna and I set the boombox up in Corey's room when we got home. It took some rearranging of his furniture, but we succeeded in it eventually. We were sitting on his bed and listening to one of his various albums. I proposed an idea I'd often considered, but had never made a point to announce. I hadn't brought her to my most cherished spot yet. I felt that after her gift today, she deserved to see it.

"You know what? I think I have a surprise for you today, too," I announced spur of the moment, after Childish Gambino ceased to play.

"Well, I'm excited," Anna grinned and latched onto my arm.

"Feel like walking?" I tried to gauge her energy.

"I love walks," Anna submitted readily.

"Let's go then, love," I offered my arm for her to take. Before we left, I swiped my old CD player from my room. Anna then gladly linked arms with me and I led her down the stairs and out of my house. It wasn't dark yet, but it probably would be by the time we got back. I knew she might've had reservations about mixing graveyards and the dark, but I could make it quick.

"I'm really glad you liked Corey's boombox," Anna mentioned as we milled down the sidewalk.

"It's still crazy to me that you took it upon yourself to get it," I turned to her. "You know? Because it's not your thing. You wouldn't feel like you have to, but you did it anyway."

"I thought it would make you happy. I love to make you happy," Anna attempted to make light of it. "Plus, I'm sure it's not just gonna sit there and collect dust. You like to listen to music too, so, why not? It's for both of you."

"You make me very happy," I gave back and kissed her cheek. I was loving her up today. "And yeah, we can have great dance parties with that thing."

"I'm not gonna lie... I was totally looking forward to that, but I didn't wanna say... Just in case..." Anna laughed that beautiful laugh of hers and leaned into me. "But now that that's out of the way, expect me over like every single day now. We're gonna blast it."

"I'll have to start buying more albums. The ones we have aren't really dance party material," I played along.

"I've got a couple to get us started," Anna smirked and began dancing to herself as we walked. Her hips swayed to nothing and she started to move her arms to whatever melody was in her head. Limbs were flailing and I was laughing.

"I love this song," I added and joined in her mini dance party. The prelude for what was to come, apparently. I waved my arms and suddenly became light on my feet. There we were on the middle of the sidewalk: being silly. Being free. No regard for anything whatsoever save each other. It was so lighthearted and chaste that I almost forgot the reason we were out here at all.

As we approached, I got an inauspicious feeling about coming here with her. I was planning on taking her to Corey's grave. It was a proposal I'd made several times internally but had always talked myself out of. I'd always feared that taking her there would put her in an awkward position. I didn't want to subject her to my tears or make her feel obligated to console me, especially not after the wonderful day we'd had. I also never wanted to bring her because I thought that maybe she would feel weird about it, or that she wouldn't know what to do. It was a sacred place to me and I never liked the thought of her not appreciating it, although that reasoning seemed far fetched.

Well into our journey, I began to second-guess myself again. The only reason we were going now was because I'd made the decision, spur of the moment. I just jumped up and went without giving myself time to psych myself out. I realized too late that she might not have been comfortable with going to a graveyard, and that I probably should've told her where we were going before I brought her along. Some people had qualms about that sort of thing. But we were almost there now, and I really wanted to share the last secret I had with her – which wasn't necessarily a secret.

"Are we going to the graveyard?" she asked as it came into view a little down the way.

"Yeah, is that okay?" I questioned nervously. I was definitely doing things backwards.

"Yeah, it's fine..." Anna nodded. Her brow furrowed, and I sensed her apprehension.

"You don't have to if you don't want to. Are you sure it's okay?" I pressed as I came to a stop.

"Yes, Jamie," she emphasized with a nod. "If you're willing to take me there with you now, there's no doubt that I'm going. I know what it means to you, and the fact that you're willing to take me – Of course its okay, of course I want to."

"Okay," I mumbled and couldn't shake that strange feeling plaguing my gut. Maybe it was because I'd never invited anyone here. It had always been a rather personal, intimate experience. Having Anna in on that made me feel like I was being exposed, although I couldn't place why.

Anna sensed the lingering apprehension I still felt and guided me into a gentle kiss. Her thumb brushed over my cheek after she connected our lips and maintained eye contact with me. "I mean it, Jamie. But we can turn around if you're not ready yet."

"No, I'm ready," I insisted, although half of me wanted to take her up on that offer. I'd much rather do away with the seriousness and bring our impromptu dance party back.

"Okay," Anna accepted my answer and squeezed my hand symbolically. Tentatively, I led her to my brother's grave. I walked the path that had become all too familiar to me, but this time I was accompanied by my girlfriend. Her hand clutched mine even tighter as we approached it.

For once, I didn't have a plethora of tissues to wipe my tears and running nose. His grave wasn't blurred by incessant tears of grief. I wasn't stricken with guilt or self-condemnation.

My knees weren't weak and my hands weren't shaking, as they usually would've been. I felt strong standing here. Anna was so cautious as she stood next to me. She was trying to gauge my reaction. I knew she was ready to comfort me as soon as I broke down. But I wasn't going to do so.

Corey's death was an unfortunate accident that could have possibly been avoided, had I given him the money. But I didn't. I'd tortured myself over that fact for long enough. Crying had never changed the reality that my brother was indeed, dead. Standing before his grave now, I was finally able to accept it in all of its glory.

Something about Anna's presence provided some clarity. She'd always told me that it wasn't my fault. I usually tried to honor that perspective, but I relapsed some days. Some days were more trying than others. But right then and there, I made my decision to wholeheartedly believe her. Not only was I making my decision, I was making a commitment to keeping that mindset. I would no longer blame myself. I would no longer be kept awake, tortured by the nagging demons in the back of my mind about this situation. I would no longer relive the image of the car colliding with my brother. I was going to put it behind me. All of it, for good.

I gently removed my hand from Anna's and crouched down. Anna crouched too, placing a steady hand on my back. I faced her with a sad smile, and she looked like she was on the verge of tears. Seeing her shed tears would make me follow suit, but I didn't want to cry. That wasn't what I came here to do. I'd done that enough. I retrieved the CD player from my jacket pocket and placed it in front of the tombstone. I placed it on the edge, along with his headphones. Then I pressed play and stood up.

Anna stayed down in a stupor. She was looking up at me with tears in her eyes. Her lips were parted as she stared at me.

"There was once a time you couldn't even say his name without breaking down and – just – *hating* yourself... And seeing you here now, without tears or anything, is just amazing. I am so proud of you," she expressed as she stood up to wrap her arms around me.

"I guess I've just overcome that part of my life. I really am ready to move on from this," I shrugged as I embraced her. "And now, it's almost like I have."

"You have no idea how happy I am to hear that," Anna's eyes sparkled.

"What you did earlier... It didn't even make me sad. It didn't really make me miss him. I didn't feel bad at all, and I don't know why. You know how sometimes, you don't notice things changing? But one day, you just look around and you're aware that everything is different?" I pitched to her and grabbed both of her hands.

"Yeah," Anna seconded.

"Being with you feels like that. Obviously, I notice that I'm happy and all... But it doesn't feel like anything about me and how I see things has changed. Until suddenly, here I am: content, with a girlfriend, speaking to people, thriving in all of these different environments. When I think about it, it all comes down to you," I elaborated. "You're the common link between it all, babe."

"It's not all on me," Anna tried to downplay her achievements regarding my progress. "I'm glad you're seeing things differently, though."

"I just – I wanted to bring you here because I think this is the last time I'm gonna come here for a while. I think sharing this moment with you speaks volumes, because *you're* the one that helped me get over this..." I emphasized her significance.

"Give yourself a little more credit," Anna admonished me, and it was so typical of her.

I paused to gesture to my position. "No. I couldn't do it on my own. I've had more than enough time to move past it, but I never did. I always tortured myself about it because that's what I thought I deserved for living when he'd died. I wouldn't *let* myself move on... Until I met you. This is the result of *you*, babe. You're the reason I'm standing here right now, not crying – Well, trying not to..." I said as one tear escaped. But even those weren't tears for Corey. He wasn't the reason I was getting choked up. It had everything to do with Anna. Reflecting on the impact she'd had on my life had moved me to tears.

Anna reached up to wipe it, then she closed the distance between us. Her arms settled loosely around my neck and she pressed her lips against mine softly. She was beginning to tear up as well, but I didn't want her to.

"I'm not even crying because of him. I'm overwhelmed because – Just thinking of what you've done for me is just so – I just love you so much... I still feel like I owe you so much, A-L..." I succumbed to my emotions and sobbed, once I started putting everything into perspective verbally. I could hardly believe that someone cared that much for me. I'd spent so much time believing that it was a hassle to love me and that I wasn't necessarily worthy of unconditional regard. I was much too much. No one had the time or inclination to support me through my strife, except for Anna.

"Stop, you don't owe me anything," Anna modestly disagreed. She never wanted to take credit for the role she played in changing my life. In saving my life.

"Anna, I might've been dead right now if it wasn't for you," I said bluntly. She never liked for me to talk about my darker thoughts. She never liked for me to verbalize the things that used to cross my mind. She never liked to envision where I could've been if we hadn't met, but sometimes I just had to paint the picture for her. "I could've been right there, next to him."

"Jamie..." Anna shuddered at the thought. She shook her head to rid herself of the concept. She always rejected that part of my history, but it was real. It still happened, and it could've been a reality if it wasn't for her.

"I know you don't want to hear it, but that's the truth. I always downplayed it whenever we talked about it, but... I wanted to die every single day, because I thought that was what I deserved. I genuinely thought that that was what I needed to do. I thought it was the only way for me to stop feeling so horribly all the time – And you changed that for me," I continued shakily, despite the obvious burden I was causing Anna with it. "*You're* the reason I've come this far... *You're* the reason I'm able to stand here without bawling my eyes out over what I *thought* I did to my little brother. *You're* the only one that changed my mind."

"Please stop," Anna closed her eyes and wiped her face. "I can't even think about that."

"I'm only saying it because I need you to know that you really saved my life, Anna," I emphasized and resigned. "I'm so thankful for you."

Anna looked at me and pursed her lips. She seemed like she didn't want to believe it, because she didn't want to acknowledge that I was once that bad off. Wordlessly, she stepped forward and pulled me into her arms. I clutched her body and hugged her securely. There was no way that I could repay her for what she'd done for me.

"I love you," she promised against my shoulder. She was stroking along the length of my spine as we stayed in an extended hug. I cherished the moment.

"I love you, too," I replied with the same amount of sincerity. She made me glad that I'd decided to stick around. She embodied everything worthwhile that life had to offer. I was thrilled that I was getting to experience it. "And now, I don't want to die at all. I don't even think about it anymore."

"Good. I want you to be happy," Anna met my eyes with her own teary gaze. A slow smile played on her lips as she looked at me.

"I am. You make me happy," I mirrored her smile and let my hands fall to her waist. "I want to wake up every day so I can spend more time with you. I want to see what every day will bring us. I want to live on so I can love you, and so I can be loved by you."

"God, you're cheesy," she denounced the sentiment. "But yes, I think we both look forward to that," Anna seconded and leaned in to kiss me again. It was the sweetest kiss I'd ever received.

When we parted from that meaningful contact, I exhaled and tuned back into my surroundings. Corey's grave was below us. I looked down at it, then back up at my girlfriend. She latched onto my arm supportively. I felt that we were just about done here, but there was one more thing I needed to express.

"This marks an ending to one tragic part of my life, and a new beginning with you," I concluded with a smile. "And you know... One day, I'm gonna die too. I'll end up in a grave, just like Corey is right there. But I'm not scared of that anymore. Because I'll get to say that I loved you, Anna Labon. And that's the pleasure this life has blessed me with. I can die happily knowing that I got to fall in love with you."

Anna's eyes softened tremendously when I finally articulated the extent it went on my end of our mutual confessions. "You mean it?"

"Yes," I affirmed and brought her hand to my lips. When I lowered it back down, we heard thunder overhead. We both looked up at the sky, then back at each other.

"It's gonna rain," she announced the obvious dopily, like she always did.

"Maybe we can beat it," I projected hopefully. Anna took me by the hand and we ran.

We didn't even make it halfway before it came down. Anna screamed when she realized she had nowhere to go to escape it. It wasn't going to help anything – we were already getting wet – but I pulled off Corey's beanie and placed it on her head to shield her. She laughed and reunited our hands. We continued to run.

I felt that it was rinsing me of my past. As the rain beat against my back and against my face, that's exactly what it felt like. Anna was holding my hand through it all as we ran, like she was leading me into this new era herself. For the first time in my life, I thought that I'd felt the rain. I succumbed to this precipitation and let my compunctions absolve with it. When it ceased to fall, I was going to emerge a new woman – with the woman responsible for my transformation. It was no coincidence that the sun was also on the horizon. A new era was surely beginning as I kissed the old one goodbye. Anna was guiding me there, full speed.

Epilogue

It took two years for Sara Bareilles to go on tour again. Jamie had gotten her first two years of college under her belt and I'd tackled my first year. Things were still going well between the two of us. In fact, we were probably the most consistent couple I'd ever seen. It was all love, all the time. Of course, we clashed. However, it was never debilitating and we always found common ground in the end. That was inspired by my parents' divorce. I was determined to work through my issues with anyone. In some ways, I was grateful that they'd split. It taught me more about perseverance.

Jamie had just called me to say that she was on her way over. I hadn't been doing anything save moving back in with my dad after going to a school in Savannah. Jamie and I decided to attend the same school after I heard her speaking so highly of it. Moving in and out of college was quite the hassle.

"Hello, love," Jamie still greeted me affectionately, despite how long we'd been at it.

"Hi," I hugged her and invited her inside.

"Boy, do I have something for you," Jamie exuded excitement as she closed us in and skipped over to our living room.

"You have something for me?" I repeated, then made note of the envelope she had in her hand. Perhaps I'd overlooked it when she arrived.

"Yes, and you're gonna love it," Jamie wore a grin that took over her features.

"Well, what is it?" I questioned and moved to sit beside her on the couch, but she giddily pulled me into her lap instead.

"Here," she handed the envelope to me and settled her arms around my waist. It had some weight to it. I wondered what was inside.

Curiously, I opened the envelope and pulled out a notepad I hadn't seen in ages. I looked at it once, then up at her blankly. "You stole my notepad?"

"No – Well, yes – Just open it," Jamie nudged me in the side.

So, I flipped it open. Memories came swarming back and it brought a contented smile to my face. This was the same notepad I'd used to speak to Jamie two years ago. I read over our conversation and laughed at how that was once what we'd had to resort to. "I remember this."

"Keep reading, babe," Jamie rested her chin on my shoulder as she read over me. So, I did.

Did you like the song I showed you yesterday?

Yes, My Love is one of my favorite songs.

You knew it already?

Of course.

Really? I thought I was sharing a secret gem.

There are no secrets, just gems, when it comes to me and Sara Bareilles.

"I remember all of this," I skimmed over it fondly.

"Okay, you don't have to reread the whole thing... But just read this," Jamie grew impatient and flipped a page or two over. She pointed to the last page we'd written to each other.

When she's back in town, we'll go together. How's that?

I would love that.

"Okay?" I laughed when I read over it again and refreshed my memory.

Jamie flipped to the back of the notepad. Taped to the back cover were two tickets for Sara Bareilles. It all made sense, then. "Are you serious?"

"I told you that we'd go together," Jamie beamed at me even broader.

"*Jamie!*" I shrieked and turned around to squeeze her. "You really mean it?"

"Yes. We're going to see Sara Bareilles in three weeks," Jamie received me and shared my excitement. She let me rock her from side to side and I might've hugged her a little too aggressively, because she pulled back from me. "Are you excited?"

"Yes!" I answered and eased up. I simply straddled her lap and settled my arms around her neck. "Wow. This is gonna be amazing. Oh my God."

"We have to go to Atlanta, though. I don't know if you want to make it a round trip or not," Jamie informed me once the initial excitement faded.

"No, we don't have to. We can stay, if you wanted to. We can stay at my mom's house," I assumed. "I can take you to all of the fun places in Atlanta, like the Georgia Aquarium and the Coca Cola Factory and Centennial Olympic Park and everything."

"Oh, yeah. I was thinking we'd have to find a hotel and stuff. I forgot about that. Wow, that makes everything so much easier," Jamie smiled at me and ran her hand through my hair. "That sounds like so much fun. Count on it."

I leaned forward and captured her lips with my own and could barely kiss her properly because I was smiling so. Jamie smiled against me as well. We were all giggles and lips against one another. "I'm so excited, oh my God."

"I figured you would be. I'm excited, too. I can't wait to go to Atlanta again," Jamie leaned back against the couch and looked up at the ceiling.

"I can't wait to finally see *Sara Bareilles*," I emphasized and fell to the side dramatically. I covered my face with my hands and squealed to myself. "Babe, I don't even think you understand."

"I think I've got a pretty good idea," Jamie responded smugly. She was so proud of herself and her gift.

"God, I didn't even know she was going on tour," I eyed our tickets and ran my finger over them.

"Yeah, it's not like she just released her new album or anything," Jamie deadpanned and I rolled my eyes.

"I know, but like – It didn't click that a new album meant a new tour. It doesn't always mean that for some artists, so," I argued and dismissed her chastising.

"All that matters is that that's *exactly* what it meant for Sara. And that we're going to see her," Jamie digressed and squeezed my side as she reiterated the fact.

"This is so cool, Jamie. Seriously, this is awesome. Thank you," I turned to her again with our tickets in my hand.

"You're welcome. There's no one I'd rather go with," Jamie graced me with a gentle kiss on the forehead.

"These next three weeks are gonna be hell," I slumped against her, impatient already.

And hell, it was. Every day, I woke up and crossed a day off of my calendar. I was always one day closer to seeing Sara Bareilles live. Jamie told me that looking forward to it so much would only make the time go by slower. Maybe she was right. I didn't care about any of it after the fact, because those three miserable weeks of waiting had finally paid off. Her concert was tomorrow and I was at Jamie's house, watching her pack last minute.

"I don't understand why it takes you so freaking long," I complained as I watched her, sprawled out on her bed.

"*I* don't understand why you packed so long ago," Jamie countered distractedly as she tried to fit her clothes into her suitcase.

"So I wouldn't have to be doing what you're doing, now," I said, unimpressed, as I crossed my arms.

"Shut up," Jamie feebly shot back as she tried to round up her toiletries. "I just don't know what I'll want to wear. I want to have options."

"You wear the same thing every day. It's not that hard to pick out an outfit. Get a tee shirt and some jeans and you're good to go," I gave a flat reply. It felt like watching her be so indecisive only made the time tick on slower.

"I do not," Jamie challenged me and put her hands on her hips in offense. Jean-clad hips. Like she usually had. Proving my point.

"Baby, we're seeing her tomorrow," I ignored her and rolled over, marveling at how time had gone by.

"I know. You've told me," Jamie said calmly. "Ten times."

"It just keeps hitting me. I've known this whole time, but now, it's actually happening. Tomorrow!" I emphasized.

"You need to go to sleep, bundle up all of this energy, and save it for the concert, tomorrow," Jamie advised me as she zipped her little bag she kept her toiletries in.

"Oh my God, it's *tomorrow*," I repeated, just to be annoying.

"I am never buying you another concert ticket ever again," Jamie said lowly. I didn't know if she was being sarcastic or not. I hoped for the latter.

"I'm just kidding, but come on. Aren't you just about finished?" I asked with thinly veiled impatience, myself.

"Yeah, actually," Jamie nodded and closed her bag and put it up next to mine against the door.

"Finally," I groaned in appreciation and rolled to one side of the bed.

"Come on, let's go to sleep. We've got a big day ahead of us, and we have to wake up early," Jamie said maternally as she turned off the light before retiring to the bed with me.

She climbed inside and curled around my body and was asleep shortly after. I didn't know how she could just readily go to sleep when I was vibrating with anticipation. It was buzzing within me. I tried not to toss and turn much with her right there, attached to me. But I couldn't contain myself. I'd stared at our tickets and tried to imagine our seats and where exactly in the venue we would view her from. Jamie had gotten us really close. I was grateful that Sara Bareilles wasn't a big name, because otherwise, we might not have gotten so lucky. Better than her seats before, we were third row. Seats E and F. I could've exploded from the sheer rush of adrenaline I felt when I thought about it again. For Jamie's sake, I tried to reel it in.

The next morning when the car was all packed and we'd said our goodbyes, I decided to present Jamie with a surprise of my own. It wasn't much, but I'd burned her a CD to accompany our road trip. Jamie offered to take her car because it had better gas mileage, having gotten over her fear of driving. She'd postponed getting her license since Corey's accident, but we built her up to it when I visited over Christmas break of my senior year. My dad had taken it upon himself to teach us both. We'd both gotten our licenses on the same day. I was the first to get a car. It was a graduation present from my parents. Jamie got one a little later down the road, which we'd just loaded our bags into.

"Ready to go?" Jamie asked me after she'd closed the trunk. She hoisted herself into the driver's seat and pecked me on the lips.

"All set," I smiled pleasantly and revealed my mixtape. "Here's our playlist."

"Is that from Small Wonder?" Jamie assumed as she took it from me and flipped it to see the back cover.

"Nope," I answered evasively.

"Who is it?" she questioned as she scrutinized it, then distractedly reached to put her seatbelt on.

"A bunch of our favorite artists. I made it a few days ago," I shrugged it off and put on my seatbelt too.

"Oh, now I'm excited," Jamie poised herself and started the car.

Jamie agreed to drive the first two hours and I said that I could drive the rest of the way if she got tired at all. It wasn't nearly as boring or tiresome as the other road trips I'd been on. Usually, I just went to sleep. But with Jamie, I had a blast. The mixtape I'd made was a mix of songs we both really liked. It prompted a lot of off-key singing, restricted seat-dancing, and using water bottles as microphones. When we tired of singing and our voices grew hoarse, we merely sat and let the radio fill our ears. The journey from Savannah to Atlanta was mostly highways and freeways. There wasn't much traffic at all, except the eighteen-wheelers we passed every couple of miles. The broken white lines were blurring together after the first hour and a half. The muted gray of the road that had once been shiny, black asphalt was making her sleepy. She kept yawning and repositioning herself. There wasn't much to look at, save the never-ending railing along the road and the dull, unappealing vegetation behind it. The trip droned on and wasn't as much fun anymore. I took over eventually and we switched when she stopped for gas.

When we neared my mom's house, Jamie came alive once more. She'd taken a brief nap to revamp herself, but had woken up when we were about thirty minutes away. The last minutes of our journey imitated the first, once more giddy with what was to come. Jamie and I sang soundtracks to Disney movies the rest of the way, and we were belting out Mulan's *I'll Make a Man Out of You* as I pulled into the driveway of my mom's house. My mom met us outside and stayed at the door until I parked.

"I've been nervous ever since you left. I kept thinking every single car was you," my mom laughed as she pulled me into a relieved hug. Jamie stood to the side awkwardly, but my mom didn't allow that at all. She coaxed Jamie into her arms as well and made it a group hug.

"It's good to see you again, Jamie," my mom squeezed her shoulder once we'd bowed out of the hug.

"It's always nice to see you, M-L," Jamie greeted her and I laughed. It always tickled me that she'd adopted a similar nickname for my parents, too. Over time, she'd started calling my dad: D-L. It was her shorthand version of Daddy Labon. She'd done the same with my mom and had dubbed her M-L for Mama Labon. She was ridiculous.

"How are you both?" she asked after she'd let us go.

"Tired," I shrugged. The last stretch had taken quite a bit out of me. The concert wasn't for another few hours and I figured I could squeeze in a nap, somewhere.

"Hungry," Jamie said concisely. I was too, despite the way we'd been snacking the whole time.

"Well, how's this? I can take you somewhere for lunch, if you're not sick of being in the car just yet," she offered sweetly. I'd missed being around her.

"I think we should probably take our stuff out of the car first," I suggested, knowing we wouldn't want to do anything on a full stomach but lay down.

"Good idea," she agreed and I gestured for Jamie to unlock her trunk. We didn't have much, just one suitcase each and a drawstring bag of Jamie's. She'd brought along a camcorder. I hadn't used one in ages, but it would make for a better video. I was sure it was a knickknack Corey would've loved.

We trekked to my room and placed everything down on the floor. My room was exactly as I'd left it. Jamie had only been here three times. Most of the time we spent together was up in Savannah. Nevertheless, there was nothing new to see in here. We dropped our suitcases off and followed my mom to the car. My mom treated us to Chili's my favorite restaurant. We ate heartily and caught up with one another. It was only two o'clock by the time we left, which meant that the concert was still hours away. When we got back home, I sprawled out on the couch and fell asleep against Jamie while she was watching a show on Netflix. When I woke up again, it was only three thirty.

I wasn't quite sure which wait was more insufferable between the three weeks and the few hours we had to wait on the day of the concert. Everything I attempted to do to waste time seemed to amount to nothing more than mere seconds. Time had never moved this slowly before. I finished the SAT faster than this. Restlessly, I cuddled up with Jamie and uninterestedly watched whatever she was watching. By six, I showered and changed into the outfit I'd been planning for a while now. Jamie was content with wearing exactly what she'd traveled in.

"Don't you want to dress up?" I tried to convince her. I looked good after putting in some effort. Jamie looked fine – she was always pretty – but I wanted her to complement me. I wanted us to look good together.

"It's gonna be dark, babe," Jamie commented as she laid on the bed, gazing impassively at me. "No one will notice what we look like, anyway."

"I know, but still," I mumbled and tried to pull my shorts up to fit my waist more properly.

"You look beautiful," Jamie compensated for her refusal to change by blowing me a kiss.

"Thank you," I blew her one right back.

"I'm gonna get them to shine the spotlight on you, just so Sara can see how amazing you look," Jamie said and got off of the bed to stand beside me in front of the mirror. She turned on the flashlight on her phone and shone it on me. "My Love."

"I would freeze, honestly," I grinned at the thought of it. "Imagine if she actually saw me. Jamie, even if she just *looked* at me – my life would be complete. She's just the most amazing person."

"I'll try not to be offended," Jamie joked.

"Love you," I turned around slightly to press a kiss to her cheek. "Oh my God, wait. What time is it? We should go."

And so, we went. I was jittery as Jamie covered the forty-eight-minute drive. I didn't know if it was the autograph kind of occasion, but I brought my journal for her to sign nonetheless. I was drumming my fingers along the binding as we came nearer. When we were in the vicinity, we attentively scanned the buildings to find the venue. We found it and it took another twenty minutes for us to find adequate parking. It was stressful for someone as impatient as I was. Waiting,

waiting, waiting. We had to wait in line to get our tickets scanned in, then we had to wait as everyone milled around the venue, buying merchandise and snacks – wasting time. Then we had to wait for someone to escort us to our seats just in case we mistakenly took someone else's. Then we had to wait for all of her opening acts to finish. I didn't come here for them. I just wanted Sara to come on stage already.

"Babe, oh my God," I shook her shoulder excitedly during the last intermission. "Oh my God, *oh my God*, it's happening. She's *actually* here. Oh my God, *we're* actually here. We're in the *same place* right now. Holy shit, Jamie. I can't believe I'm actually-"

I was shut up by her gentle kiss. She grasped my cheeks and slowly coaxed me into silence with her lips against mine. By now, my heart rate had increased significantly, but for an entirely different reason. In the dimly lit venue, I saw how much amusement her eyes radiated. Her thumb brushed over my cheek and she kissed me one more time. "I know, babe. You talk way too much, but you're so cute."

"Sorry," I laughed and subtly leaned into her touch. "I've just never been to her concert before, Laur."

"I'm glad I'm here with you. This side of you is definitely new," Jamie grinned at me, yet to remove her hands from my face.

"I'll definitely regret this later. I bet you'll hold this over me forever," I predicted with a halfhearted scowl.

"I just might bring it up on a rainy day," Jamie smirked. "You know I'll have to tease you all about how - *oh my God, we actually* went to the Sara Bareilles concert," she mocked me with a much higher pitch.

"You're the worst," I laughed despite myself and pushed her gently in the shoulder.

"You love me," she refuted confidently.

"I do," I affirmed and leaned forward to capture her lips again, but the lights dimmed. And I think I may have accidentally screamed in her face.

I wasn't the only one screaming. Seemingly all at once, the crowd went crazy. Everyone lost it. If I wasn't so excited, I probably would've been covering my ears. It was so loud. The love for Sara Bareilles was extremely palpable throughout the massive crowd of people. Everyone adored her. Everyone was here for her, and she hadn't even come out yet. When she did, however, it only got more intense.

Song after song, I found myself screaming the lyrics right back at her. I was having the time of my life. Jamie, not so much. I knew she was having fun, but she was rather subdued. She was moderately enjoying herself. While I was freaking out, flailing myself all around and singing awfully all the same, Jamie had taken her idle position next to me. Jamie was too detached from the scene for my taste – I wanted her to dance with me. However, that wasn't really her style and I didn't hold it against her. She was taking in the atmosphere as much as I was thrusting myself into it. She could appreciate it all from right there in her seat while I felt the need to express myself more vividly. That was okay.

During *Gravity*, however, she got up and hugged me from behind and sang along quietly into my ear. She was definitely in a cuddly mood tonight, contrasting how I was practically bouncing off of the walls most of the time. That was one of the few slow songs of the night, then Sara Bareilles picked up the tempo again and Jamie left me to have my own fun once more.

Every so often, I would grab Jamie's hand so she could jump and dance around with me. She gave in and did away with her reservations long enough to follow my lead. For the second half of the concert, we fist pumped and frolicked in place as one. Jamie had just started to get into the vibe itself when the ending of the set list approached. *Brave* was the song that made my girlfriend the least restrained. Side by side, we screeched along to Sara's flawless performance and practically exhausted ourselves. I was just glad Jamie found a way to experience it like I did. After the encore, and once it was all said and done, and Sara had vacated the stage, and the crowd started to disperse, I only turned to Jamie.

"That... Was the best thing ever," I expressed hoarsely, having lost my voice after the concert. "Thank you so much. I love you, I love you, I love you."

"I love you, A-L," Jamie happily retuned and kissed me between my eyebrows. "Come on, baby. Let's get out of here."

The concert was everything I'd hoped it would be. Sara Bareilles was brilliant. Her raw talent shone on the stage as she slayed her piano. Magic flowed from her fingertips as she accompanied herself. She hit every note. She played every chord with dazzling perfection. Her interactions with the crowd were so genuine. We laughed. I cried. Sara sang with so much conviction and passion. There was so much love within the atmosphere. It was just as Jamie described it – a sea of people coming all together and singing with their favorite singer. And I was there with my favorite girl.

Made in the USA
Columbia, SC
19 July 2023